MATILDA'S RETREAT

CATHERINE CAVENDISH

ISBN 978-1-63789-347-0
Macabre Ink is an imprint of Crossroad Press Publishing

For information address Crossroad Press at 141 Brayden Dr., Hertford, NC 27944
www.crossroadpress.com

Cover by GetCovers

First Edition

To Colin

who believes I can

Lynn

1997

Chapter One

"Bloody hell, Lynn. How much further is it?" I could feel my husband Pete's patience draining the more we bounced up and down on the unsurfaced road. That's if you could call it a road. It barely qualified as a lane, as it meandered uncertainly up, down and vaguely across the heathland.

Not that I could offer much comfort. "I've never been here before either. Terri and Keith only bought the house six months ago."

Pete's fingers gripped the steering wheel as we hit yet another deep rut. "One more like that and I swear the bloody rear axle's going to snap."

Given my husband's lack of knowledge of anything mechanical, I hoped he was wrong, but our poor little Nissan was hardly built for this terrain. Terri and Keith had acquired a Land Rover. Now I could see why.

We bumped and bucked our way another half mile or so when I let out a whoop of joy. "It's over there. Look. Just off the road, to the left." I jabbed my finger at the windshield.

"Okay, okay. Just off the road? You mean there's something worse than this?"

I didn't answer. My full attention had been drawn to the edifice built on a slight incline. It was huge—mansion proportions. It stood there, master of all it surveyed. Built of local stone which had blackened over the years, the building looked sturdy enough to withstand anything the harsh local climate could throw at it and, as this was the heart of the Pennines, in a remote part of Yorkshire, that would be plenty. Gales, snow, lashing rain. This house seemed to challenge it. It was a house built to be defiant. But there was something else. It looked hostile, unwelcoming and…secretive.

I told myself to stop being ridiculous. Fortunately, at that moment, I caught sight of something much more familiar. "There's the Land Rover, parked right outside. Look, it's Terri. She's waving at us." I opened the window. "Hi Terri," I yelled, but the wind caught up my words. She was making circling gestures with her hands. "She wants you to drive round to the side. Maybe it's easier that way."

Pete grunted and attempted to wrestle the steering wheel away from its stubborn determination to use a newly discovered deep rut as a sort of rail track. Finally with a couple of extra-large bumps we ground to a halt, and the engine sighed as if thanking some automobile deity that its present ordeal was over. Goodness alone knew how we were going to make it back onto the main road. Maybe that rear axle really would snap. I made a mental note to ask Keith and Terri to escort us. That way if we got into difficulty, they would be on hand to bail us out.

I opened the passenger door and the wind hit me with such force, I couldn't breathe. "Wow, is it always like that?" I managed after a few moments of gasping. "I mean, last time I looked it was July. Anyone would think it was winter."

Terri laughed and helped me to my feet while her long red hair blew around her like a flowing halo. "You get used to it." She raised her eyes heavenward.

"Sometimes it helps to walk off-kilter," Keith said. "You know, bent a bit to one side, leaning into the wind or whatever. It's great at night here though, with a howling gale raging outside, whistling down the chimneys while you're all tucked up in bed, or curled up in front of a blazing fire. We love it here, don't we Terri?"

Terri's expression was one of resignation rather than enthusiasm. "Oh yes, Keith. We love it here." Her wry smile surprised me. From our phone conversations I had gathered she really liked this house.

Keith frowned, then clapped his hands together. "Come on, grab your stuff and let's go inside. Mulled wine and that roaring fire will soon thaw you out."

I followed Terri, with Keith and Pete bringing up the rear.

"It's the car I'm worried about," Pete said. "It's no spring chicken. I had no idea you were this isolated."

"It didn't seem like it when we bought this place," Keith said. "Besides, we wanted somewhere away from the city. Terri fell in love with the house as much as I did, so that was that."

Given the expression on Terri's face a few moments ago, I doubted that was still the case. No doubt I would find out the truth over the weekend.

The front door meant business. Built of solid oak, it looked original. The sign chiseled into the stone above it read 1767 and that seemed entirely right. When Terri turned the heavy iron ring that served as the door handle, it opened with a satisfying clunk and creak of old hinges in need of some oil.

"I must deal with that," Keith muttered as we trooped in.

The hallway was unexpectedly large, with a stone-flagged floor and an ornate iron chandelier which would once have held candles but now sported authentic-looking electric lights concealed in Gothic lampshades. Doors led off left and right, while straight ahead a sweeping staircase, with magnificent balustrades, stretched upward. At the top of the stairs a triptych of stained-glass windows that looked as if they had once graced a cathedral, grabbed and held my attention. "So beautiful," I whispered.

Beside me, Terri squeezed my arm. "Rather special, aren't they? They were originally in Talamund Abbey, about three miles from here. It's an old ruin now but apparently it was quite something in its day. Mind you, it had its fair share of scandal."

"More than its fair share, I'd say," Keith said, "if the stories are to be believed."

"Oh? And what stories are those?" Pete asked. My husband always loved a juicy scandal.

"Save it for later," Terri said. "Right now, you two look as if you need that mulled wine. I'll show you up to your room and then I'll go and pour us some. Brewed it myself."

Our room was off to the right at the top of the stairs. Another substantial door revealed a bedroom which had once been sumptuous.

Exquisite molding adorned the ceiling and upper reaches of the walls that were otherwise painted a shade of pale blue-green, sadly faded and peeling. A dusty chandelier that, if restored, gave all the promise of glittering crystal, took center stage, suspended from the ceiling by a substantial chain. Beneath our feet, a somewhat threadbare, traditionally patterned carpet partially covered floorboards that showed signs of having been meticulously polished back in their day. More tall windows, with floor-to-ceiling dark blue velvet curtains that bore witness to the perils of long exposure to sunlight, while a massive bed complete with Georgian-style mahogany bedside cabinets completed the décor. Reading lamps had been added, their style attempting—mostly successfully—to blend in with their extravagant, if dilapidated, surroundings.

"Sorry about the state of the room," Terri said. "We're living in a work in progress, I'm afraid. That's why this place was so cheap. That and its location, I suppose. At least the mattress is new. We only got it last weekend."

"It's fine, Terri" I said. "We came to see you, not the furniture."

Her brilliant smile lit up her face, but I couldn't help thinking she seemed to be forcing it. Pete meanwhile was staring out of the window. "Bleak out there, isn't it? Looks like Kate Bush could come running over the moors at any moment."

I joined him and linked my arm in his. He was right. Gray clouds swirled overhead, and a few drops of rain turned into a torrent as the wind whipped it up into a frenzy so that it lashed the windows. If this was a summer storm, I dreaded to think what a winter one would look like. In the distance, a half-ruined tower commanded my attention. "Is that Talamund Abbey over there?" I asked.

"Yes. Not much left of it now." Terri came to join us. "Only that tower and a few crumbling walls. I went up there once with Keith. Such a creepy place. I felt like I was being watched the entire time we were there. I'll tell you some of the legends about it downstairs."

I shivered and tore my gaze away from the ruin. "I wouldn't want to be out in that storm right now," I said. "Lucky we missed it."

She touched my arm. "I'll get that wine ready for you. Don't be too long; it's best drunk hot."

"We won't," I said and took off my jacket. I looked around in vain for a wardrobe. There were two doors apart from the one by which we had entered. I opened one. Bathroom. Presumably integral to this room. I moved to the next and turned the handle. "Bingo." I grabbed a clothes hanger from the odd assortment hanging on the rail. My jacket safely stashed away, I unzipped the weekend case.

"Best leave that," Pete said, as he turned back from the window. "I can't abide cold mulled wine. Come on, let's go down."

Terri was as good as her word. We found our friends ensconced in Regency-style armchairs either side of a roaring wood fire that crackled and gave off a considerable amount of heat. She thrust steaming mugs of hot wine fragranced with cinnamon, orange and an assortment of spices into our hands. Pete and I sat next to each other on a well-upholstered sofa in that same eighteenth-century style that seemed to be the way Terri and Keith had decided to take the house forward. Soon warmed by the fire and pleasantly lightheaded after two gulps of the wine, I kicked my shoes off and tucked my legs up onto the sofa. I felt the soothing mellow warmth of the drink flow through me.

"So, tell us the stories then," I said. Terri looked blank. "About Talamund Abbey."

"Oh, yes."

Strangely, Keith shot Terri a look that almost screamed, *don't say anything*. I didn't know him all that well despite him being married to my best friend for ten years or more. Living in different parts of the country, we only saw each other once every year or so and then not usually for long.

Terri ignored her husband's look and leaned forward. "I looked Talamund Abbey up on the internet, and it was a really odd place right from the start. It was supposed to be a strict Trappist type of order, but in fact its adherents were followers of Afagddu ap Llewellyn, a former Welsh monk who had the dubious distinction of being burned as a witch. Until he was accused and brought to trial, Afagddu had founded and led a community of around two hundred monks and built Talamund Abbey to house them all back in the early 1600s. Rumor had it that the devil himself provided the wherewithal, even building the abbey with his own hands, but it's far more likely that Afagddu had a benefactress—a besotted female follower. Anyway, the monks were said to be devil worshipers and around fifty of them also burned at the stake for their heretical practices. The rest fled. No one would go near the building for a generation or more after that as it gradually fell into ruin, all except the west tower with those windows and a few bits of wall. The stained-glass was stolen, but the structure of the windows remained intact within one of the remaining sections of wall. When the builder of this house came along and saw them, he decided he must have them. He commissioned new stained-glass and the result is what you see today."

The fire crackled, breaking the silence that had fallen as Terri told her tale. I cleared my throat. "If only those windows could talk."

Terri nodded. "Exactly. What stories they could tell, couldn't they, Keith?"

Keith drained his mug and swallowed before speaking. "It's all a load of hokum. She'll tell you about the ghosts in a minute. Don't believe a word of it."

I unwound my legs, set my empty mug down and sat up. Beside me, Pete looked as if he were about to nod off. The long drive up here from Somerset had taken its toll, no doubt.

"What ghosts?" I asked.

Terri seemed to be well and truly settled into her subject now, whatever Keith might or might not think of it. "Well, I've done some research and it seems there are a couple, maybe more, that haunt this house. It's known locally as Matilda's Retreat, but the name refers to an earlier house built on this same ground. We don't know much about Matilda except she is believed to have been resident here in the early sixteenth century. Then there's the link to Talamund Abbey. She's supposed to have been a particularly close follower of Afagddu and probably his lover and benefactress. She's the besotted female follower I mentioned. She never married but is rumored to have borne a child who died in infancy, possibly as a result of being sacrificed by his father."

It didn't take much to work it out. "So Afagddu had an illegitimate son with this Matilda, and then killed him?"

Terri nodded.

"Absolute rot," Keith said, and stood. With rather more vigor than necessary he chucked a log on the fire, sending sparks flying.

"Careful, Keith," Terri said, "You'll set the carpet alight."

A slight smell of singed wool drifted up my nose. A tiny ember glowed a few feet from me. Keith stamped it out.

"Stop filling Lynn's head with this paranormal babble," he said, and he really didn't need to sound so angry. In a matter of minutes, Keith had transformed from an affable husband. For some unaccountable reason, he seemed to be blazing with rage.

Terri's face showed a mixture of embarrassment and annoyance. "Oh, come on, Keith. It's just a bit of fun. Every old house should have its share of ghost stories, true or not. Isn't that right, Lynn? I haven't upset you, have I?"

I leaped to her defense. "No, of course not, and I agree. This house couldn't possibly have passed its two hundredth birthday without something haunting it."

Keith pointed at my husband from whom gentle snoring noises rumbled. "You've bored Pete to sleep anyway."

"He's driven over two hundred miles today," I said. "And the last few weren't easy." Okay, I was probably over-reacting, but I really didn't care for the way he was speaking to Terri.

Keith glared at me but said nothing, went over to the drinks cabinet, opened it and poured a generous measure of brandy into the appropriate glass.

Behind his back, Terri mouthed *ignore him* and I nodded. But the whole exchange bothered me. If this went on, we weren't in for the pleasant relaxing weekend both Pete and I craved. We had both been working flat out for months without so much as a day off. Running our own small publishing company was sheer hard work, even if we did love it. Maybe we should have rented that little cottage in Devon that Pete had been so drawn to. Me and my big mouth!

Pete gave a sudden lurch and opened his eyes. He blinked at Terri and then me. "Oh, I'm so sorry. Must have nodded off there. Did I miss anything?"

Terri smiled. "Only my husband being a complete idiot," she said. Keith slammed his drink down and strode out of the room. The door banged shut behind him.

Terri's eyes filled with tears. Instinctively I went over and put my arms around her.

"I'm so sorry," she said. "Keith's not been himself recently. Not since we moved here. I mean we can go days, sometimes a week without any problems but then suddenly it's as if a switch clicks on and he becomes this…I don't know what to call him. Like a stranger, but not a friendly one. He gets so angry and…"

"Has he ever hurt you?" I asked. "Physically, I mean."

Terri hesitated a second too long before shaking her head.

"You can tell me, you know," I said. "We've been friends forever after all."

"Thanks, Lynn. But…. You know, I loved this house when we first saw it. Didn't hesitate when Keith suggested we buy it, but now I wonder if we shouldn't sell up and move back to the city. There's still a lot of work to be done here and we probably won't get back what we've sunk into it but at least maybe we'll keep our marriage."

"Have you mentioned this to Keith?" Pete asked.

"No, you're the only ones I've told. I'm probably being stupid and I'm sure Keith's right about the stories. Pure hokum. But there's something…. I can't put my finger on it. An atmosphere maybe." Terri stood and went over to the drinks cabinet. "Damn, Keith drank the last of the bottle and I could do with a brandy. I'll fetch another one from the library. Everything's so topsy-turvy here but we've been working on the kitchen and moved a lot of stuff out. We've yet to start on that room."

"I'll get it," Pete said and left us.

Terri took a couple of tumblers out of the cabinet. "Do you fancy a drink? There's no more mulled wine, I'm afraid. Oh, hang on, I never told Pete which room's the library."

At that moment, Pete returned, brandishing a bottle of Courvoisier. "Here we go. That's a lovely room, Terri. Won't need much doing to it once you've redecorated."

Terri took the bottle from him and proceeded to pour our drinks. I declined. By now, my stomach was signaling it needed replenishing and a delicious smell had wafted in from the kitchen when Pete opened the door. Terri must have smelled it too.

"Oh heavens, the casserole. I must get the potatoes on. I made a Boeuf Bourguignon so it wouldn't matter what time you arrived, but you must be starving. Please excuse me and I'll get things moving."

"Can I help?" I asked.

Terri was already at the door. "No thanks. Everything's under control." She smiled and left us.

From my perspective I felt things were far from under control. "That was awkward," I said.

Pete sighed and sipped his brandy. We both sat back down on the sofa and gazed into the fire for a few moments, each lost in our own thoughts. Then something struck me. "Found the library all right then?"

"First door I tried. There were bookcases lining every wall so I guessed I was in the right room and, sure enough, there were the bottles on a small table. Brandy, wine, rum, whisky. You name it, they've got it. Maybe that's the problem. Keith's taken up drinking."

"If that's the case, I can't see that selling up, taking a loss and moving will do the trick."

"Maybe not." Pete lapsed into silence again.

Presently, Terri opened the door. "Dinner will be ready in about fifteen minutes. We'll eat in the dining room. It's not too bad in there."

Pete and I stood. "Enough time to go and unpack," I said, and the two of us made our way to our room.

A few minutes later, unpacked and more than ready to eat, we descended the sweeping staircase. Pete led the way. He made straight for the door on the far left of the hall.

"Which is the library?" I asked.

"That one." Pete indicated the one immediately to its right, in between the one he was now standing in front of and another room we hadn't explored yet.

"Terri just said the dining room was next to the library. She didn't specify whether it was on the left or the right."

"Trust me, Lynn. I know these things." He winked at me, opened the door and sure enough there was the dining table laid out for four people.

Keith was already seated drinking a glass of red wine. He stood up as we entered, a sheepish look on his face. "I must apologize for my appalling behavior earlier," he said. "It was so rude of me."

"No harm done," I said, wishing I didn't feel the rush of animosity that now flooded me. Had he abused my friend? If she rolled up her sleeves, would I see bruises on her arms? I swallowed hard and sat down as far from him as the small circular table would allow. It wasn't nearly far enough. Pete took the seat opposite me after giving my shoulder a reassuring squeeze.

Keith passed the half-empty bottle of Margaux to me, and I poured a small quantity before passing it over to Pete.

Terri brought in a sizeable casserole dish, laid it down and removed the lid. The rich aroma of Bourguignon enriched my senses.

"Get stuck in while I fetch the vegetables." She handed me the oven glove. "You'll need this."

"Let me help you," I said, standing.

"No, no, Lynn. I can do it. You're our guest. Sit down and help yourself."

I did as she requested, sat down and helped myself, before passing the serving spoon to Pete. Keith was in the process of practically emptying the casserole onto his plate when Terri returned with mashed potatoes and broccoli. Seeing her, he returned the laden spoonful he was about to add to his plate back into the serving dish.

I picked up the oven glove and slid the dish over to Terri. She said nothing, merely nodded her thanks at me. Meanwhile, her husband was tucking into the vegetables like a greedy schoolboy. Had he always had such gross table manners? I tried to remember the last time we had all sat down to a meal together but no memory of it would come to mind. Why should it if there had been nothing to note about it? Surely, I would have remembered such blatant greed. The unedifying sight made my stomach muscles clench and my appetite waned. I spooned a small amount of potato and broccoli onto my plate and tasted the beef. The meat melted in my mouth. Delicious. "Fabulous casserole, Terri."

I said and then stared pointedly at Keith. "Your wife is an excellent cook, isn't she?"

"What?" Now he was speaking with his mouth full. At least he had the grace to stop cramming in forkfuls of food long enough to chew, swallow and reply. "Oh yes, excellent." I glanced over at Terri. She looked as if she might burst into tears at any moment and, despite the small amount of casserole that remained for her to eat, seemed to have no appetite for it. I saw her take two forkfuls. The rest of the time she merely pushed her food around before laying her knife and fork together.

Pete cleared his plate while, I, put off by the repeated noises of Keith belching like a pig in a trough, only managed to finish my casserole. The vegetables remained untouched. "Sorry, Terri. Everything was wonderful but you defeated me. Now please let me help you clear up or I shall feel useless. In fact, I think all three of us should do the washing up and let Terri have a rest after all the trouble she's gone through. What do you think, Keith?"

"Oh, Keith doesn't do housework," Terri said.

"What? Whyever not?"

Terri shrugged. "It's not his thing."

"Well, it's his thing to live in the same house and eat your delicious food so, as a 'thank you' at the very least, he should do some chores. Pete does."

Keith's response was a chortle of derision that made me want to slap him.

Pete kicked me lightly under the table and gave an almost imperceptible shake of his head. I hated it but I supposed he was right. Their domestic arrangements were their own affair, and I had no right to challenge them. In any case their marriage appeared to be under enough strain as it was without me adding to their woes.

I settled for, "Come on, Pete, let's do the washing up."

Keith's expression was one of disgust as he watched Terri and the two of us clear the table while he continued to sit.

Out of earshot and in the kitchen, I turned to Terri. "Has he always been like this? I mean, this is almost the twenty-first century. He's behaving like a relic from the Fifties. Maybe earlier. He's like Henry the Eighth, sitting there guzzling and belching."

Terri sighed. "He's never been one to willingly grab the vacuum cleaner, but he always did his bit, with a little nudge from me. Since we moved here though.... Before I knew where I was, I was doing everything myself. At least he pulls his weight with the renovation work. He loves it. His pet project is the library. As Pete will have seen, but was too polite to mention, it's a total wreck at the moment but, as he said, the walls are lined with bookcases—just like a stately home. Keith reckons it's going to be spectacular when he's finished with it. Apart from that, we use professionals for the specialist stuff but other than that, he really gets stuck in. We're fortunate to be able to work from home, like you two. We couldn't live here if we didn't. Our internet auction site is going well, so workwise and financially everything's fine. It's just our personal life that's totally fucked. And I mean totally."

She didn't have to spell it out. I knew what she meant. Keith chose that moment to join us. "I'm going into the living room now," he announced. Pete dried his hands on a towel. "They've got you well trained," he said, his voice the embodiment of a sneer.

I held my breath, but Pete had evidently decided to choose good manners over indignation. He said nothing. Keith left us.

Throughout the rest of that awkward evening as we sat in the living room, Keith spoke little, periodically topping up his drink. From wine at dinner, he had now reverted to brandy and was busy making inroads into the new bottle Pete had found in the library.

Terri seemed fidgety and ill at ease—a world away from the smiling figure who had greeted us on our arrival. From time to time her eyes would dart toward the door as if expecting someone to walk in. I longed to get her on her own to probe more into what had gone wrong between her and Keith, but the opportunity simply didn't present itself. Pete was clearly struggling to keep his eyes open, and, by midnight, he had lost the battle.

"Come on," I said, gently pulling him to his feet. I smiled at Terri. "I think the combination of all that driving, good food and wine has taken its toll. Night, night, sleep well. See you both in the morning."

Keith continued to stare into the fire as he had for most of the past two hours. Terri put her arm around my shoulder and gave me a light kiss on the cheek. "I'm sorry," she whispered.

I nodded and smiled. "It's okay. We'll talk tomorrow."

If Keith had heard any of that he gave no sign. My "Goodnight, Keith" was met by a perfunctory wave.

We mounted the staircase, and I had the sudden sense of someone coming up close behind me. I glanced over my shoulder and almost overbalanced. I grabbed hold of the rail to steady myself. There was no one there and Pete continued to trudge his weary way up the last of the stairs. The slightest of breezes brushed my cheek, raising goosebumps on my arms. I felt sure someone whispered in my ear but the sensation was gone before I could properly identify it.

Pete turned to me. "Coming?"

I nodded, stroked my cheek and carried on up the stairs, keeping a firm grip on the handrail.

Up in our room, Pete wandered into the bathroom while I changed into pajamas. When he emerged, yawning widely, I pulled back the covers. He slid in under the duvet. "What is it with Keith?" he asked. "Sullen bugger, isn't he?"

"Yes. There's something I can't put my finger on. Don't you find this house…" I searched for the right word. "Disturbing?"

Pete's response was a gentle snore.

I brushed my teeth and joined him in bed. It probably took me all of two minutes to fall asleep.

Chapter Two

I don't know what woke me, but it was still pitch dark. I listened. The wind whistled and howled, occasionally rattling the windows. Then I heard another noise. It could have been the wind moving up a gear, but the moaning sound seemed to be coming from somewhere in the house. Somewhere not far from that room.

I grabbed my dressing gown from where I had slung it over the bed. Tying it securely around me, I slid my feet into my slippers and made for the door. The moaning was louder now. Much closer. My first thought was Terri. What if Keith had taken out his anger on her? After all, I knew she was lying when she told me he had never hurt her.

I didn't hesitate. I opened the door and stepped out into the dimly lit hallway. I turned to the right but could see nothing. Only shadows that deepened the farther along I looked. I didn't even know which room was Terri and Keith's.

To the left, a few yards away was the landing. Straight over that was another wing of the house. At some stage during the evening, Terri had mentioned that they hadn't so much as looked in those rooms yet and were concentrating their efforts on getting one half of the house straight before tackling the other.

The moaning came again. There was now no question of where it was emanating from. I made my way to the landing. Precious little light seeped through the massive windows but, as I passed them, I felt a chill so deep it seemed to penetrate my bones. Then, it seemed to pass straight through me, leaving a residue of sadness, and a feeling of utter wretchedness that made me want to sob my heart out. Tears tracked down my cheeks, and I wiped them away with my fingers.

The moaning was almost on top of me. I stopped, hardly daring to breathe. I was now part way down the unexplored wing. Some of the doors were open allowing moonlight to illuminate patches of the corridor before plunging me back into almost total darkness. I could no longer hear the wind, but it couldn't have died down so fast, surely?

Ahead of me, a light started as a wispy, iridescent cloud, gently twisting in a languorous, almost sensuous fashion before settling into a more defined and recognizable shape. Draped in an old-fashioned nun's habit, the woman's face shimmered silvery-white under her wimple, and her eyes were closed as she drifted toward me. I tried to move back but my legs wouldn't work. I wanted to cry out, but my vocal cords froze. She was no more than two feet away from me when she stopped. Her habit billowed out behind her even though there was no breeze. Around her neck she wore a crucifix. The face of the Christ was stuck in an expression of pure agony as blood dripped from its eyes and ran in rivulets down its body, mingling with the blood from its hands, feet and pierced side. Its mouth was open as if caught in mid-scream.

The nun's claw-like hands clasped together in a gesture of prayer that seemed more like a mockery. The crucifix twisted around on its chain until it was facing downward. The nun's eyes flashed open. Still unable to move, I mentally flinched from the piercing gaze of two bright yellow, feral orbs. In a second, a door slammed shut and a rush of wind slammed into me from behind. It shot through me and struck the nun. She let out a hideous cry like a wounded wild animal, baring shark-like teeth. Some invisible force flung her backward, away from me, down the corridor where her shape once more transformed into a cloud before disappearing.

Suddenly all was quiet. No moaning. No wind. I found I could move again and took an uncertain step backward. I screamed as hands caught me before I fell.

"It's all right, Lynn. I'm here."

"Pete, oh thank God. It was awful."

I let him cradle me in his arms as he led me back to bed. Only when he had tucked me under the duvet did he question me. "Whatever happened? And what were you doing there?"

I told him about the moaning, the nun and all that occurred in those impossible minutes. He heard me out, only speaking when I finished.

"That must have been one hell of a nightmare. I suppose it was all Terri's talk of the ghosts that are supposed to haunt this place that brought it on."

"What? *Nightmare?* It was no nightmare, Pete. What I experienced was real. You must have seen her. Or at least that weird cloud thing."

"All I saw was you, standing there. Then you staggered back and almost fell into my arms."

"Well, yes, that's true but that was because of what had happened to me. There was a cloud and it transformed into a hideous nun. I'm sure it wanted to kill me, but I couldn't get away. I couldn't move. And there was another…ghost or something. It passed through me. Twice. I think the second time it may have actually saved me. It seemed to be some kind of force for good against that…that *thing*. I don't know who or what that nun was, but she was no Christian. I'm sure of that."

Pete got into bed. "It's late. Sleep on it and see how you feel in the morning."

The trouble was, with everything that had gone on and now Pete challenging what I had seen, sleep was going to be well-nigh impossible for the rest of the night.

I gave up trying at around six, got up and had a quick shower. Pete was always a heavy sleeper and today was no exception. I left him and made my way downstairs in search of a cup of coffee, only to find Terri had beaten me to it. A cafetière stood on the kitchen table in front of her as she sat, staring into her mug. She looked up when I entered.

"Couldn't sleep either?" she asked, and I noticed the dark circles under her eyes. Devoid of makeup she looked ten years older than she had the previous day.

I shook my head. "Have you ever had any strange experiences here yourself?"

Terri took a sip of coffee before answering. "Some. Why? Did something happen during the night?"

I told her. Unlike Pete I could tell that what I was saying resonated with my friend. As I finished my account, I said, "What's going on here, Terri?"

Terri sighed, and it seemed to come from the depths of her very soul. "Okay, enough's enough. I know this must all seem crazy to you. I thought with you two here, it might help. I thought Keith might pull himself together and if I made an effort to be the way I always used to be we could get on an even keel again... But it's no good. The truth is, Lynn. I'm scared stiff. At first, I thought I was imagining things. That I was dreaming. That's when I started doing research on this place. We had only moved in a week or so earlier, so it didn't take long for things to kick off. The first time, I had an almost identical experience to yours, only I made my own way back to bed, convinced I'd had a waking nightmare.

"The next morning, I told myself that it really hadn't happened, but it kept niggling at me, so I researched more. That's when I found out about the origin of the landing windows, Matilda and Afagddu. She was devoted to him, but he was evil through and through. I gave you the sanitized version last night because Keith gets so angry otherwise. Don't ask me why because I have no idea. All I have are my fears that somehow this house has possessed him in some way. I've learned that there's contemporary evidence Afagddu took Matilda's money for his abbey. He made her his mistress and then persuaded her to offer up their newborn son as a sacrifice to Lucifer. He imprisoned her here—in her own house, for heaven's sake. His sect practiced ritual sacrifice on a regular basis. Babies, innocent young girls...you name it. It was a bloodbath.

"Nuns from legitimate orders occasionally visited, thinking they were paying a courtesy visit to fellow sisters in Christ. Needless to say, they never made it out of here or of Talamund Abbey. At least one of those nuns is supposed to haunt here. And then there's Matilda herself of course. She is rarely seen apparently, but maybe that's who you saw last night."

"The nun with the inverted crucifix?"

"It would fit, and, despite her appearance, she wasn't ever a real nun although she always wore a habit. Once the abbey was built, Afagddu's following grew at a fast rate. The monks came from actual orders to which they were patently unsuited. Most of them had only taken holy orders because their families made them do it. Minor sons of the gentry and so on. They were drawn to him for the debauchery he encouraged and took on his evil ways with relish. With their support, he went on for a number of years, doing exactly as he chose until an abbess reported three of her nuns missing. One by one other abbesses reported similar cases and when these were added to local stories of abduction, missing children and reported instances of satanic rites, the church decided to investigate. The rest I told you. Matilda and Afagddu were burned as witches and heretics."

"So, she haunts here still. Is *he* around?"

"I bloody hope not. Haven't we got enough trouble?"

Her attempt at a smile didn't work. I poured coffee for us both. It was lukewarm but it didn't matter.

"Yesterday you said you were thinking you and Keith should sell up and leave here."

"Yes. You saw how he was. He was never like that before we came here. Right now I'm married to a stranger…" Her voice tailed off and her expression changed to a wide-eyed stare.

I followed her gaze to the door where Keith stood, leaning against the frame, looking disheveled, unshaven and generally hung over. "You two are up early," he said, his lighthearted tone at severe odds with his appearance.

"We both had insomnia," I said. "So we're doing a bit of catching up."

Keith nodded and shuffled to the fridge. He took out a carton of milk and proceeded to drink straight from it.

"Keith, please," Terri said. "Use a glass."

He stopped drinking long enough to scowl at her before resuming his drink. The carton empty, he crushed it in his hand. "No point now, is there?" he said and tossed the carton in the direction of the kitchen bin.

He shuffled off again, scratching his head.

Terri retrieved the carton and stuck it in the bin he had missed by inches. "I'm so sorry, Lynn. This is another thing about him. He always had impeccable manners but now…"

"You don't have to apologize for him," I said. "He's old enough to know what he's doing."

"But that's the point." Terri took her coffee mug to the sink and emptied the contents. "When he's like this, I don't think he does know what he's doing. He's possessed. Look, I know it sounds far-fetched, like something out of a Hollywood horror film but it's the only way I can explain it."

I nodded. After my experience, who was I to argue?

It all happened in an instant. A series of thumps. A resounding crash. A scream of agony. Terri and I raced out of the kitchen into the hall. Lying at the foot of the stairs, his legs at an unnatural angle, was Keith and he wasn't moving. Terri cried out and ran to him. I stood immobile for a few seconds; certain I had seen a shadow flash through the hall.

Pete called from the top of the stairs. "What's happened?"

Terri sobbed and cradled Keith's head in her lap. Pete raced down the stairs, his dressing gown flying around him. I knelt down beside Terri. Keith's sightless eyes stared up at us, his face twisted in an expression of agony that reminded me too closely of the crucifix around the ghostly nun's neck.

"Call an ambulance," I said. Pete, his face ashen, nodded and raced back up the stairs. Moments later he called down from the landing.

"Where's your phone?" he asked. "Mine's completely dead."

"What?" I struggled to remember. "It's in my bag. You'll see it."

Pete dashed off. Terri was rocking Keith and keening. Tears flowed freely down her cheeks, and she gasped for breath between sobs. I put my arms around her and let my own tears flow.

Pete was back. "Yours is dead too. This is fucking impossible. Terri? *Terri.*" She paused mid-sob. "I need your phone."

"Kitchen," she managed. "On …the…table."

Once again, Pete appeared; this time he was shaking Terri's phone. "None of the phones work. I don't get it. What the hell are we supposed to do now?"

This seemed to drag Terri out of her present torment. "It's happened before. Neither of our phones would work even though they were fully charged. The laptop won't work either. Nothing electronic will and, as for the landline…" She picked up the nearby receiver and listened for a second before holding it out. "Listen for yourselves."

I took it from her. Instead of a dialing tone there was a high-pitched whistle that hurt my ears. I handed it back. "What *is* that?"

Terri shook her head. "No idea. Telephone engineers have come out twice but it always works while they're here. Ten minutes after they've gone, it goes back to this."

"But, why?" I had a horrible feeling I knew the answer.

"This house. When it's had enough, everything will work again."

"We need an ambulance *now*."

Pete felt for the pulse in Keith's neck. "I hate to say it, but I don't think it will matter too much *when* the ambulance arrives."

Terri wailed. "No, no. He can't be…"

"I'm so sorry," I said. Pete knelt with us and put his arms around Terri and me.

A few moments later he spoke. "I can't wait around here. I'll take your Land Rover and get to the nearest neighbor."

Terri raised her head. She swiped at her tear-soaked cheeks. "There's no one for miles in any direction. There isn't even a telephone call box. Not one that works anyway. The nearest police station is ten miles away in Carrswick. You go back to the main road and turn right. The road takes you straight into the town."

"I'll find it. You stay with her, Lynn."

As if I would leave her; but I merely nodded.

"Where are the keys?" Pete asked. No response. "Terri, I need the keys to the Land Rover."

"On… On the hook, by the kitchen sink."

"You'd better put some clothes on," I said.

Pete looked down at himself and dashed up the stairs. Five minutes later he was dressed and, keys in hand, he left us. Presently the sound of an engine revving signaled his departure.

I eventually managed to coax Terri away from Keith. She leaned heavily on me as I led her into the living room where the ashes of last night's fire lay cold in the fireplace. Without the comforting blaze the room felt chilly, inhospitable and held a musty odor that wrinkled my nose uncomfortably. I shivered and settled Terri down on the sofa. I covered her with the throw that lay over the back of it. Luckily it seemed to be made of pure wool and looked warming as I tucked it around her. She seemed lost in her own tragic world and barely noticed what I was doing. Despite the early hour, I made for the drinks cabinet and poured her a stiff measure of brandy which she accepted from me and drank deeply. It seemed to help, if only a little.

"Please, Lynn. Please get a blanket and cover Keith. His face..."

"Of course."

"You'll find a linen chest in our bedroom. It's two doors down from yours on the same side. There are blankets in there."

I left her and went into the hall. I picked my way carefully around Keith's body and ascended the staircase. Above and ahead of me, the landing windows glinted in the early morning sun. After last night's rain, the rays of light cast a rainbow of reflections into the house. It should have been a breathtaking sight. And it was. But not for any artistic reason. Silhouetted in front of the middle window, directly in my path, stood a figure and I knew it was *her*. Matilda. My stomach did a somersault and bile shot up into my throat. She spread her arms wide and vanished as if she had never been there.

I paused, my left foot on one step, my right on the one below. My hand gripped the carved stair rail. I told myself what I had seen was a mere trick of the light, caused by the refracted rays of sunlight. Right then I wished I had paid more attention in physics classes at school. There was something about prisms and bending light wasn't there? Or maybe I had imagined it.

The house was silent. That should have reassured me. It didn't. This was an unnatural silence. I forced myself to carry on to the top of the stairs where I made my way to Terri's bedroom and located the linen chest. There must have been at least half a dozen blankets in there and I pulled out three. The place seemed to be growing colder by the minute and if things carried on like that, we would need one each at least. Then there was Keith's body. Could a fall have resulted in that expression?

Or had what Keith saw right before he died have been the cause of it? Did something or someone push him down the stairs?

Matilda.

I tried to push my fears away, but they kept returning, all the way back down the stairs where, once again, I felt a presence close up behind me. I quickened my step while taking care not to trip. With my armload of blankets that wasn't easy, but I made it to the ground floor where I covered Keith with one, relieved that I could no longer see those staring eyes which refused to stay closed. I dared to peer over my shoulder. Nothing there. I couldn't feel it now either. I glanced at my watch. Pete had been gone fifteen minutes, so with any luck he would be back on the main road by now and on his way to the town. At least he was driving the Land Rover, which should make light work of the local terrain.

Back in the living room, Terri had a little more color in her cheeks and gave me a weak smile when I joined her. "I'm sorry it's so cold in here," she said. "The central heating works but, like everything else, it needs renovating. In fact we are…were…planning to install a whole new system." She stood. "I'll sweep out the ashes and build a fire." I could tell she was doing her best to calm down. Maybe doing normal, mundane things like this helped her.

"What can I do?" I asked. "Do we need more wood?"

She nodded. "If you don't mind getting it. There's a wood store outside. You turn left out of the front door and follow the wall round. You'll see an outbuilding and it's in there. You'll need the bucket." She pointed to a sizeable wooden pail set at the side of the fireplace. "Put the gloves on or you'll get splinters."

I did as she suggested, picked up the bucket and left her sweeping up piles of ash. I made a slight detour to collect my phone which Keith had left lying on the kitchen table next to Terri's.

The air was considerably warmer outside than in. A rush of it hit me as I descended onto the path and took deep, refreshing breaths. Its sweetness provided a marked contrast to the stale, heavy atmosphere that clogged everything inside the house they called Matilda's Retreat. Some retreat. It had to be an ironic nickname, didn't it? There was nothing restful about that place. Keith may have only just died and in the most tragic and sudden way, but the sooner Terri was out of that house the better. I resolved to persuade her to come back with us—but then who would make all the necessary local arrangements? There was nothing for it; I would have to stay on with her. In the wood store, I reached in my pocket for my phone and switched it on, relieved when it instantly sprang into life. Seventy-five per cent charged. But equally as quickly, the screen went black again. This time it wouldn't revive, as if something was blocking the signal.

I shoved my phone back in my pocket and collected enough sawn logs to fill my bucket. I then needed both hands to heave it out of the outbuilding, across the yard and back into the house. Terri appeared at the door of the living room.

"I'll help you," she said.

Between us we lugged the wood into the living room where the neatly prepared fire awaited us. Terri had rolled up newspaper and added kindling and she now lit it. Once it got going, she proceeded to add a couple of logs. Before long she had established a warming blaze.

I checked my watch again. It was now over half an hour since Pete left. "With any luck he should have reached the police station. Is your phone working yet?"

"I'll check."

A few minutes later Terri had still not returned from the kitchen, and I went in search of her. I found her in the hall, bending over Keith. At my approach, she straightened and threw back the blanket over his face. "I still can't believe this happened," she said. "Keith. Murdered. In his own home." She pointed up the stairs, a sudden, wild look in her eyes. "Look. Can't you see her?"

I gasped. The nun was back. Silhouetted as before so that I couldn't distinguish her face, but it had to be the same entity. This time, her arms were folded in front of her. I could make out her white hands, locked in that prayer-like gesture—a mockery of anything holy and sacred. All around us, the air grew thick, musty, tasting sour and bitter.

"She's…come…for us," Terri said, panic making her gasp her words.

Not you.

The voice came from within my head. A guttural, female voice.

"Did you hear that?" I asked.

Terri looked at me blankly "Hear what?"

"That voice…" But I knew. It had only been meant for my ears.

In a heartbeat, a dark all-enveloping shadow swept down the stairs and wrapped itself around my friend. She began to choke, her eyes bulged.

I cried out, tried to get to her, to help her, but the shadow resisted all my efforts. It knocked me backward and sent me hurtling across the hallway where I hit the wall and collapsed in a heap on the floor.

Chapter Three

"Lynn. Lynn. Can you hear me?"

I opened my eyes to see Pete's anxious eyes peering down at me. My brain felt as if it was smothered in a blanket of fog. Everything echoed. I didn't recognize where I was except it was clearly a hospital bed. I was wired up to a drip and, as I shifted position, a sharp stabbing pain deep in my abdomen told me I was catheterized as well.

I tried to sit up, but my back protested. I remembered being thrown against the wall and hoped I hadn't done any lasting damage. At least I could move my legs and wiggle my toes. I could feel the sheet against my skin. These were good signs, weren't they? The fog lifted a little in my head. "Where's Terri? The last thing I remember she was being attacked by some...I don't know what."

Pete moved to one side, revealing a female police officer standing there watching everything, hearing everything.

"What happened to Terri?" I asked again, fearful of the answer. "And why are the police here?"

Pete looked at the police officer. She nodded.

"I'm so sorry, Lynn. There's no easy way to tell you this. You've been in a coma for nearly twelve weeks. When I got back from the police station that day, I found you unconscious and Terri... She died, Lynn. She was already dead when I got there. She suffered an aneurysm. They said it would have been almost instantaneous. She wouldn't have suffered."

I shook my head. "No, no. That's not how it was. That...*thing*...was strangling her. Terri was choking. I saw her eyes... That was no aneurysm. I mean, I'm sure it wasn't. She was murdered. Like Keith. Something in that house..."

"I'll get the nurse," the police officer said and left us.

"What's going on here, Pete? Why is *she* here?"

"The doctors could tell you were coming out of the coma, so the police have come to interview you. You see, Terri's death has been ruled as down to entirely natural causes but there remains a question mark over Keith. I've given my version of events, but I didn't see the accident."

"Neither did I. Assuming it *was* an accident."

"But you can verify where Terri was at the time he fell. I can't."

Pete settled me back against the pillows. The shooting pains in my back eased a little but surely after three weeks any bruising should have healed. "What have I done to my back?"

"You've slipped a couple of discs. Nothing that can't be fixed. It's going to be a bit uncomfortable for a while but they're confident you'll be fine. They'll start physiotherapy now you're back with us, and lots of walking, maybe a bit of manipulation, that sort of thing."

The door opened and a female nurse with a friendly smile entered, accompanied by the female police officer and a male colleague.

"How are you feeling now, Lynn?" the nurse asked as she pulled on a pair of latex gloves.

"I suppose I'm quite good considering I've been in a coma for twelve weeks."

"Excellent. We'll do your obs.—temperature, blood pressure and so on—and then I'll leave you with these police officers for a bit. We'll be able to get you off the drip and take the catheter out later too."

The male officer held the door open for her and the three of them left.

"I suppose I have to do this now. I've come out of a coma, learned my best friend has died of something that I know with every fiber of my being she didn't and now I'm expected to make a statement to the police. If I make any sense, it'll be a miracle."

Pete sat on the edge of the bed and clasped my hand. "I know it's hard, Lynn, but it's for the best. All you have to do is tell them she was with you and it's job done."

"Who's taking charge of the…arrangements?"

"I did. Her parents live abroad, and Keith's are dead. He has a sister in Australia but no other relatives. To cut a long story short, both families asked me to do it, so I did. It sounds callous but it gave me a focus while I was worrying about when, or if, you were ever coming out of that coma."

"What about our business?"

"You needn't worry about that. I've been able to look after that with some help from two bright young people Gavin recommended. You remember Gavin who helped us so much when we were starting out? He leapt to the rescue, installed those two and here we are. Making more money than ever."

I tried to smile. "And where is here exactly? I mean I know I'm in hospital but where?"

"Leeds. The doctors didn't recommend moving you too far, so I'm staying in Terri and Keith's house, and I come here every day. Then I catch up with the team when I get back. Hey, everything's going to be fine. It's terrible about Terri and Keith, but we'll get through it."

He sounded so matter-of-fact. How could he sit there and calmly tell me he was living in that house without an apparent care in the world? "But the internet…the problems with that house. The phones wouldn't work. The things that went on…" My rising panic must have been obvious. Pete made gentle shushing noises, patted my hand and my panic turned to annoyance. What was I? A petulant child?

"Everything's fine, Lynn. The internet works, the phones work and the house is … Well, it needs a lot doing to it but other than that, it's a house. Quite a fine one actually."

Were we talking about the same place? I didn't have time to pursue my concerns. The nurse returned and Pete seemed to grab the opportunity to stop having a conversation he didn't want to engage in. Maybe it was my imagination, but he immediately said he was going for a coffee and sandwich and left. As soon as the nurse had removed the drip and handed me a glass of iced water, in came the police officers and I told them all I knew. Only I didn't, of course. I merely answered their questions, signed the statement they wrote, and they left me alone. With my thoughts.

Dark thoughts.

Chapter Four

The day they allowed me to go home, I had mixed emotions. Pete had made it clear that, for now at least, "home" meant the house on the moor. Terri and Keith's house. He told me he had a lovely surprise for me when we got back.

He collected me in the Land Rover. Evidently, he was in charge of disposing of all their goods and chattels and had free use of anything in the meantime.

"It makes it easier for everyone," he said as we drove the twenty or so miles from Leeds. "I'll sell up and transfer the money into their accounts, split equally, in accordance with their wills. I had a solicitor draw up the papers, so it's all signed, legal and above board."

"What's the surprise then?" I asked.

He smiled. "Wait till we get back."

The Land Rover certainly made life easier tackling the track leading to the house. We bounced but the vehicle was built for it. Where our poor car had struggled, this one almost jumped for joy like an eager puppy, albeit given the Land Rover's twenty years, a middle-aged one.

The house loomed into view, dominating its landscape. We were approaching it from the opposite side of the narrow road and from this angle, its gloominess was inescapable. The turreted roof, multiple chimneys and windows that, far from providing the eyes of the building, served only to emphasize its dark and sinister secrets. A lump formed in my gut, and I could barely swallow. All I wanted to do was grab the steering wheel, spin the car round in the opposite direction and get out of there as fast as the Land Rover could take us. Somerset with all its green lushness suddenly seemed a million miles away.

Pete drew up alongside our Nissan and helped me out. I hobbled, leaning on my recently acquired walking stick. Three weeks of intensive physio in the rehab unit and I still felt like an old woman. Tears sprang to my eyes. No. The stick would have to go. I had made a few attempts at walking unaided, not very successfully, but this time I was determined. I handed the stick to Pete and took my first tentative steps unaided.

"Do you really think you should be doing that yet?" He laid a hand lightly on my arm.

"I need to do this, Pete."

"Very well, but I'm keeping my hand here. I can catch you if you stumble."

I nodded and concentrated all my effort into putting one foot in front of the other. It wasn't far, maybe a dozen or so steps, but my feeling of achievement when I reached the entrance was so overwhelming, I almost forgot my fear of the house.

Once inside, I was struck by the relative warmth. Outside, the day was fine, but the breeze had an icy edge to it, colder than usual for the time of year even this high up. In the house, by contrast, it felt cozy and welcoming. Not at all like the atmosphere that had cloaked it the last time I had been there.

Pete waved my stick in the air. "You won't be needing this much longer. That was most impressive." Nevertheless, he handed it to me, and I took it. To be on the safe side. He looked pleased with himself. "Come on, let's go into the living room."

I followed him in.

"Sit yourself down and I'll fetch it."

"Fetch what?"

He grinned. "You'll see."

First came the bottle of Bollinger nestling in a champagne bucket full of ice, plus two fluted glasses on a tray. Then Pete advanced to me with a cream-colored envelope. It was sealed.

I took it from him. "What is it?"

"Open it and find out," he said.

I slid my finger under the crease in the envelope and ripped it open. A single, folded sheet of good quality paper was the only content. I unfolded it, read what it said and then re-read it, to be sure my eyes weren't deceiving me. "This says we are the owners of the property popularly known as Matilda's Retreat, Talamund Lane, Altby-by-Carrswick. But that's *this* house."

Pete's face was wreathed in smiles. "That's right. I bought it. That is, *we* bought it. It's ours, as near as damn it. The building, furnishings.... This is our new home, Lynn."

I had never seen him so thrilled about anything. Words rushed into my head; none would form a coherent sentence. I wanted to shake him. More than that I wanted to shake some sense into him. "You can't seriously be suggesting we live in this godforsaken place, can you?"

"Of course. It's perfect. It's going to be wonderful, Lynn. No more city, no more hassle of crowds and people prying into your business."

"It never occurred to me anyone was. Not especially anyway. Since when did you fall in love with this house? You hated it when we arrived."

Pete glanced quickly over his shoulder although I had no idea why. "I don't think I ever said I hated it. No, I'm sure I didn't."

"You certainly weren't keen. You complained about the isolation. You couldn't understand why Terri and Keith had moved here. And, if you remember, Terri wanted to leave. She had seen things. Things that shouldn't be here...and so have I."

"Mass hysteria, that's all it was. I've been reading up about it. Terri told you ghost stories, the house is spooky, the wind was howling that night and your brain did the rest. Terri saw a ghost, so you saw a ghost. Simple as that. You fed off each other. You nearly dragged me into it too. But since Keith and Terri.... Since I've been here on my own, I've come to love this old place. We can make it into a fabulous home, Lynn. Hey, we could even have kids."

Now I knew he had flipped. "Since when did you have a craving to be a father? It was one of the first things we agreed on when we first started going out together. No children."

"I know, but we were city folk then. The city's no place to raise children, especially these days. They belong out here in the country where they can roam free and safe, with nature all around them. Idyllic."

"No, Pete."

He sighed. "Oh well, give it time, maybe you'll change your mind."

I shook my head. "End of conversation."

"Let's have that champagne."

The rest of the day and into the evening passed. He had made a casserole—his take on Terri's Beef Bourguignon—and I had to admit it was delicious.

As the sun went down and the shadows lengthened, my eyes grew heavy. Since I had come round from the coma, I found that I tired easily. The doctors reassured me this was a temporary thing and as time progressed, it would get better but, right now, I needed to sleep.

"Let's get you up to bed," Pete said. "It's been an exhausting day. Exciting though, isn't it? Our own new beautiful home."

"We *have* a beautiful home, Pete. Down in Somerset."

"Oh, I put that on the market. The estate agent's dealing with it. Within twenty-four hours we had an offer that matched the asking price and it's a cash buyer so it's going through as fast as the paperwork can be signed."

I glared at him, my tiredness evaporated by incredulity. "And you did this without consulting me?"

"I needed to move fast, Lynn. You were in a coma. I had no way of knowing when you were going to come out of it. If I'd hung on, I could have lost this house."

"So, you needed the money from our home to pay for this? *Our* home, which was in both our names. When did you get me to sign the paperwork?"

"I knew you wouldn't mind. I copied your signature."

"You did *what*?" The Pete I knew wouldn't have done that. Some stranger had moved into his body and taken over. It was the only explanation. "Well, I suppose that at least makes sorting out this madness a whole lot simpler. All I have to do is prove I couldn't possibly have signed that paperwork and the deal's off."

Pete's smile snapped off like a light switch. "You wouldn't do that, Lynn."

"Wouldn't I? Look, Pete, I don't know what's got into you, but this is utter lunacy. I'll stay here tonight but, in the morning, we are going to undo all this nonsense and get the hell out of his house. Forever. You can tell the estate agent you've changed your mind and, as for the forged signature, you can say…well I don't know how you're going to get out of that one but all I can do is prove I didn't sign it. If I come out and state that baldly, the deal is off for certain, but the police will probably get involved. It's fraud, Pete, and that's serious. You've bought this property on the basis of a fraud. That could mean prison."

"But you wouldn't do that. I'm your husband."

"And I'm your wife, the one you are supposed to love, honor and respect, but it didn't stop you forging my signature, did it?"

A gulf had opened between us, and not only had the shadows darkened in the room, but a pall also seemed to have descended. The room was shrouded in a damp, decaying and festering malodorous atmosphere that set my teeth on edge and made my bones ache. I wanted to get out of there. With all my heart, I wanted to run and never look back, if only my legs would work properly and fast enough.

I stared at Pete, the man I had known, loved and lived with since I was twenty. Fifteen years. Now when I looked at him all I saw was a complete stranger.

"What have you done with my husband?" I asked.

"What did you say?"

His voice sounded different. Only the face and body remained the same.

"You look like Pete but you're not."

He reached forward to touch me, and I flinched. My own husband who wouldn't hurt a living thing, but right now, I was scared of him.

"What's the matter, Lynn?"

"Please…keep your distance, until I figure this all out." But how could I? There were no logical, rational answers. Every question yielded a supernatural response. My mind raced. Pain or no pain, weakness or no weakness, I had to get away from here and I had to do it tonight. There was no point in trying to make a run for it. He would catch me before I made it to the front door.

I thought of the Land Rover. I had never driven one before, but it was the obvious choice. Had he returned the keys to the hook in the kitchen where Terri used to keep them?

I moistened my lips. "Look, Pete I have no idea what's going through your head or why you did what you did. Tomorrow we'll sit down and talk about this. See where we go from here. Right now, I need a glass of water. "

"I'll get it for you."

"No. I need to walk. I've been sitting too long."

I shuffled my way into the kitchen, relieved to find that after the first few steps, my joints seemed to ease up until by the time I reached my destination, the kitchen sink, I was walking with no recourse to the walking stick either. I was a bit unsteady, wouldn't be running any marathons any time soon and it bloody hurt, but at least, with Pete unaware of my movements, I had a chance of getting out and to the car. I grabbed a glass and poured cold water into it. One quick glance showed me that Pete hadn't changed Terri's habit. There were the Land Rover keys hanging from their hook. I thought for a second about putting them into the pocket of my jeans but if Pete saw them missing, he would suspect I was up to something and I could never explain what I was doing with them apart from the obvious. Reluctantly, I left them there and concentrated on trying not to limp or stumble out of the kitchen, glass in hand.

"Let's get you to bed," Pete said. "You'll feel better after a good night's sleep."

I doubted that but let him lead me upstairs to our room. It was cold in there too. It seemed the house had put on a show for me when I arrived home but as soon as it realized I wasn't buying into it, gave up the pretense and reverted to its natural hostile chill. I undressed while Pete set about unpacking my few belongings, stacking up dirty washing.

"I'll take this lot down to the washing machine once I've tucked you in. Think I'll stay up a bit. Watch some TV."

He tucked me in, kissed my forehead and left carrying my washing. I lay wakeful for ages, but must have dropped off through sheer exhaustion because when I awoke, Pete was snoring gently beside me, and a full moon was peeking through a chink in the curtains.

Taking care not to disturb him, I slid out of bed, ignoring the jabs of pain from my back and legs. I located my slippers and dragged my dressing gown off the bed.

Outside the room, the silvery moonlight pierced the stained-glass and cast multi-colored beams of light that illuminated my halting way down the stairs. At the bottom, I turned and made my way to the kitchen.

The gentle whirring of the washing machine greeted me as I crossed the floor, my legs becoming surer of themselves with each footstep as I concentrated on willing the pain away. I grabbed the Land Rover keys and, as an afterthought, pulled a raincoat I guessed to be Terri's off the back of the kitchen door. A pair of wellingtons stood on the floor right up against the fridge. I kicked off my slippers and slid my feet into them. Gently, I dragged the bolt back on the door and turned the key in the lock. Then I was outside, breathing good, clean, Yorkshire moorland air. The breeze had died down and it had turned into a chilly night. But the stillness was alarming. It felt as if it was waiting for something. I buttoned up the raincoat, grateful that Terri and I were a similar size. In the distance, an owl hooted. Dowsed in moonlight, there stood the Land Rover. Only a few more steps …

I unlocked the doors and climbed into the driver's seat. My body protested at the various contortions I had to put it through in order to adjust the seat so I could reach the pedals. I kept willing myself on and inserted the key in the ignition. Then I saw Pete in the rear-view mirror. He had the front door wide open and, as I threw the car in gear and spun the steering wheel, he started to run. He made straight for me as my foot slipped off the gas pedal. I regained control. He was almost on top of me. Panic set in. Unused to the way the car handled, I must have yanked the steering wheel too hard. Instead of veering away from him, I headed for him, my foot firmly on the gas. It all happened in seconds. I heard the thud and felt the impact of his body against the hood. His eyes were wide, staring at me as he slid off and to the side. I screeched to a halt, made to open the door and froze.

Pete was not alone.

Matilda stood over him, her eyes blazing, her nun's habit billowing behind her even though there was no wind. She raised her hand and pointed at me. I didn't hesitate.

Once more, my foot hit the gas and the car responded. I didn't look back until I made it to the narrow road. Then I glanced into the rear-view mirror. The moon must have gone behind a cloud. All was pitch black behind me. I had no idea of the time, only that it was very late. There was no traffic nor any sign of any as I turned in the direction of the long homeward journey and set off.

I had been traveling for no more than a few minutes when the road suddenly narrowed. With no memory of this when we first came up here and having approached from the opposite direction when we returned from Leeds the previous day, I was perplexed. I knew I should keep on going straight and that would take me eventually onto the ever-busy M62 motorway, but surely this road had been wide enough for two cars to pass yet it was rapidly becoming a single-track lane. All I could see was illuminated in the beams from the headlights. The occasional rabbit scurried for safety. Apart from that I was alone in unfamiliar territory. There was no doubt this was the wrong road, but how could it be? I hadn't turned off anywhere.

Then the road ended. I braked and peered ahead. No more tarmac, only moorland.

I switched off the engine, turned on the interior light and found the glove box. Inside lay the answer to my immediate prayer. A flashlight. I switched it on, and, after a moment's hesitation, I was rewarded with a strong beam. I scrambled out of the car and swept the flashlight around the landscape. To my left the light picked up something. A wall. Maybe there was a house here. Someone I could call on for help.

My back was complaining but I pressed on. The illumination revealed more of the wall and my hopes raised only to be dashed a moment later when, following the structure around its outer edge, I came up with the bad news. It *had* been a wall, but it no longer held up the building for which it had been designed. I flashed the beam upward and caught sight of a sign. I screwed up my eyes until I could make it out.

Talamund Abbey

There was more but I didn't need to read it. That was disheartening enough. I could see what was happening. I had been brought here. For what reason I had no idea although I feared the worst. All my senses quivered with the knowledge that whatever the purpose, it wouldn't be pleasant. Not for me at any rate.

In a second, I sensed movement all around me. Shadows moved; voices whispered incoherently.

Matilda stood in front of me, her hands clasped in that all too familiar gesture of some diabolic prayer; the crucifix inverted, with Christ's agonized face staring upward.

The devil ghost raised her hands, and they were bone, devoid of all flesh. She knelt in supplication and for a second it seemed she was worshiping me, until I realized there was something close up behind me. Something that stank of the grave.

"Take her." The voice was raucous, more like a crow or a raven than a human. I didn't need to turn to know that behind me stood the entity this abominable "nun" and her fellow believers worshiped and adored.

Invisible hands forced me to the ground and held me down. Matilda lay prostrate over me. How long did it take for her to do her work? I have no idea. All I know is that when it was over, I was no longer myself. Lynn Schofield and all that she was and had ever been reduced to a small speck of light within a body of darkness and hopelessness.

Matilda de Talamund owns my body. She lives again with her paramour—Afagddu. She killed not only Keith but Terri as well. Keith was her intended but when Pete came along, she no longer wanted him. Terri had to go because, without Keith, what was the point of her? I became her perfect choice of host while Afagddu...well, he doesn't live inside Pete all the time. I don't know how much Pete realizes he is being controlled. Matilda is the perfect me. She behaves as I did before any of this happened. Of course, she loves the house at least as much as Pete. As much as Pete has been conditioned to love it.

As for me, I have no voice. If I have a soul, I have no idea of its existence. Matilda is in control of my body every minute of every day and in those dark hours when Pete is sent to slumber and Afagddu claims his body, I have to endure the frantic, animalistic lovemaking.

And it has borne fruit.

Matilda is pregnant and my body will have to carry and deliver it. Pete is ecstatic. The man who said he couldn't stand children and would never have one!

But history is nothing if not prone to repetition. When this infernal baby is born, what will become of it?

Diana

2025

Chapter Five

"This is a joke, right? You are having me on. Surely. Will, *tell* me you're having me on."

The extent of my husband's smile told me all I needed to know. It extended up to—and included—his eyes. He meant it. He really had bought this place.

I switched from staring at him to staring back at the house. Around me, the raw northern wind whistled, froze my ears, aggravated my dry eye condition so that tears spilled over my eyelids and raced each other down my cheeks. The building stood silent, shabby, run down, neglected but somehow defiant.

Defiant and menacing. Maybe the weather played a part. The clouds rolled, rain-filled, gunmetal gray, threatening an imminent downpour. I could taste it in the gusts that tried to knock me over. I wouldn't let them. I planted my feet slightly apart and stood my ground. The house glared back at me through broken windows and it told me one thing. We might own it but it would never be home.

It was home to someone though. Perhaps not now. Maybe in the past. I prayed as hard as I could at that moment. Prayed that whatever had once called this godforsaken pile home had long since departed, never to return. Somehow, though, I couldn't quite believe it. Anger swelled up in me and I swallowed hard. I didn't want to shout at Will. It had been a horrible year. First his adoptive mother's illness—from diagnosis to her funeral in under six months, the cancer she had done so well to hide for so long only discovered when it was too late to do anything about it. Will, holding her hand as she lay in bed at the hospice, days away from the end.

"Why, Mum? You must have known something was wrong."

"Oh, yes ... dear," she had managed in between gasps for air. "I knew. Cancer. Had to be. Smoking ...very bad for you."

"But if you had said something earlier. Seen your doctor.... They could have operated."

"Cancer...always gets you...in the end."

"No, Mum, it doesn't. Not these days. Not if you catch it early. There's so much they can do now. Radiotherapy. Chemo.... All sorts."

"Living death."

She wouldn't have it and then, as she slipped away, Will's outpouring of grief smothered in guilt. "I should have visited more often. We should have made more time for her."

No amount of comforting would help. Not really. I tried, of course. I said the right things and my heart broke for him. And then I felt guilty too. Gail Clarke was a lovely woman—a second mother to me after my own had died so young. But work had seen us move three hundred or more miles away southwest of her comfortable Yorkshire cottage in the pretty little village, a mere twenty or so miles from where I was now standing; the same cottage we inherited, along with a great deal of money Will had known nothing about until her solicitor presented us with a copy of the will.

"Your late adoptive father was a shrewd investor, Will," Mr. Cartwright, Gail's solicitor of many years' standing, said. "He had an eye for the next big thing, bought low and sold high. Did your mother never tell you?"

I sat there stunned into silence while Will shook his head. "I had no idea. I wonder if she did. I mean, money wasn't something that was ever discussed in the family. Everything you're telling me.... I had no idea."

The solicitor sat back in his chair. "She knew all right. She told me. Soon after your father died. She was sitting right where you are now, Diana, and she said, 'That'll be for Will and Diana when I'm gone. It'll set them up for life. Then perhaps they won't have to work so hard.'"

She was right, of course. That happened three months ago and here we are. Moved into the cottage after her funeral, put our own house on the market which was then snapped up in a cash sale twenty-four hours later. A whirlwind. I hardly had time to catch my breath. We had both quit our jobs and now…this.

I dabbed my cheeks again. Damn dry eye disease. At my age I was young to be suffering with it and it was a bloody nuisance. It made me look as if I was crying. "Didn't you think I might like to be involved in any decisions to move house? We've only just moved up here to your mother's cottage. Are you going to sell that? What's going on, Will?"

He seemed reluctant to drag his attention away from the house but forced himself. "I know it's going to take money, and a lot of work, but neither of us has a job. This will be our project. I thought we could make a start here, make it habitable, and then move in. Maybe we could rent the cottage out while we finish this and then decide where we want to live and which property we want to sell."

"And when did you decide all this?"

"A few months ago."

"A few…*months*? And you never thought to tell me what was going through your mind?"

"I only really decided just before we moved up here. Then, as we were going to be living up here anyway, it seemed too good an opportunity to miss."

"So, you bought it."

"Yes. Paid cash. The paperwork is going through as we speak. Should get the keys in a couple of weeks. I didn't touch our money. This came out of Mum's inheritance and there's still plenty to live on. The place was dirt cheap. The previous owners…died."

I didn't like the hesitation there, but amidst everything else he was hitting me with, it really didn't seem of much consequence. We stood in silence, our thoughts wildly different from each other, of that I was certain. His would be happy for the first time in months and mine more concerned than I could ever remember feeling. Icy droplets of rain fell, scything down my already frozen cheeks. Now they mingled with the tears which no longer needed the dry eye condition to create.

That was the beginning. And I knew I wasn't going to relish what came after.

Chapter Six

Will was out shopping in town when I decided to make a start on the former library. We were almost ready to move in; the roof was repaired and the place was finally weatherproof. In a bathroom on the top floor, a spindly sycamore sapling had reluctantly given up its hold on an old enamel bath where it had managed to root itself in a pile of mud that had accumulated on the bottom. A family of mice had been persuaded that a life out in the wild was far preferable to a precarious existence at the back of a kitchen cupboard, and we were thanking whatever gods might be listening that there were no bats lurking in the rafters—maybe the sieve-like holes in the roof had rendered the house just too undesirable a residence for them. Had we found any, all work would have had to cease while the bat conservation people became involved. Selfish of me I know but I wanted to get the place renovated and on the market as quickly as possible.

I had decided to look on Matilda's Retreat as an investment property—one to be sold as soon as it was habitable and attractive enough to make us our money back. Any delay, for any reason, was not to be contemplated.

I thought I had become accustomed to the creaks and bangs of the place. The creaks were invariably old timbers, the bangs—unnerving at first—were down to the much-mended water pipes. Every time the toilet flushed, a cranking, clanging and groaning echoed around the building.

"It sounds like souls in torment," Will said when we first heard it.

"Victorian plumbing," pronounced the local tradesman, armed with his bag of tools and years of experience. "I see a lot of it. And it always sounds like this. Not usually quite as bad, but then…. This is a *really* old house. Maybe you've even got a bit of the old Roman stuff mixed in with it." He laughed and I felt foolish. For a moment I had actually entertained that thought. That was the problem with this house. It felt as if you were living in a mausoleum one minute and the next like some kind of time machine capable of transporting you back centuries for split seconds.

I saw things out of the corner of my eye. Things that could not possibly be there. A fleeting glimpse of a young woman, dressed in a nun's habit, a monk, tall and moving slowly, his hood lowered to cover his head. That one chilled me. Another time I thought I glimpsed a different nun holding a baby. Its face was bright red, screwed up as if it was screaming its head off, but there was no sound. I tried to tell Will. He told me to stop reading ghost stories at night. I pointed out I was reading Armistead Maupin's *Tales of the City* for the umpteenth time to take my mind off the strange surroundings he had brought us to. Will's response was to shrug, shake his head and tell me I must have dreamt it all—or perhaps I was overdue for an eye test.

I had no one to talk to here, and I really needed someone. The internet wasn't connected and the waiting list was weeks long. We were in a sort of dead zone, they told us. Cable was out of the question and there was something about the terrain that meant satellite signals were often unreliable and intermittent. Our phones only worked in certain parts of the house and then not consistently. We certainly wouldn't be advertising *that* when we came to sell.

The nearest neighbor was maybe a couple of miles away down the bumpy lane and onto the main road. A farmer, his wife and three young children. They were responsible for the sheep that wandered freely on our part of the moors. The first morning I drew back the kitchen curtains to be confronted by a ewe staring curiously at me through the window made me jump. Now I looked forward to my morning encounters. She at least listened to what I had to say, chewing away, blinking steadily.

I asked the farmer what her name was and he looked at me as if I had just landed in the Tardis. I changed the subject by offering him a cup of coffee. He settled for tea and a chocolate Hobnob—well, half a packet actually. By the time he left, I learned his name was Geoff Sutcliffe, his wife was Margo and the kids were Sam aged ten, Jacob aged seven and little Lily aged just four. He'd inherited the farm from his father and it had been in the family as far back as anyone could trace. He couldn't remember a time when he hadn't been allowed to graze his sheep on our land—or maybe he was just saying that. I suspected the latter but that would keep for now.

He also had a few tales to tell about Matilda's Retreat. He told me about a notorious Welsh monk who had escaped certain capture in Wales and set up a community at the now ruined Talamund Abbey where the nuns and monks were of dubious religious adherence. The monk's name was barely pronounceable—Afagddu ap Llewellyn—but he was also known locally as Brother Alfred.

"All the ladies loved him," Geoff said, starting on his third mug of tea. "The story goes that he was very handsome and ladies would swoon whenever he crossed their path. That's how he recruited his nuns. I don't think the Pope had much say in it, and there were a number of babies over the years...but Brother Alfred himself? Well, he only had eyes for one woman and that was Dame Matilda. The story goes she was widowed young. Her husband had been a cruel and vicious man much older than her who used to beat her regularly. But she had some money of her own and used it to build a house here. The one before this one." He looked around himself. "'Course it didn't have a name then. The folk around here christened it because here is where she would escape to let her wounds heal after the latest beating. Anyway, on one such visit, she met Brother Alfred and they fell in love. Pretty soon and under some questionable circumstances, Matilda's husband was found dead. They say his chest was caved in and there was such a look of horror on his dead face that those who found him couldn't bear to look on it."

I shivered. Goosebumps arose on my neck and arms. It seemed the room had grown darker. At the same time, Geoff shifted in his seat and set his mug down. He wiped his mouth with the back of his hand and stood. "Anyway, enough chatting, I'd best be getting back. Your husband will be back soon, no doubt. You'll have the dinner to get on. He'll not thank me for keeping him from his food."

I didn't like to enlighten him that we were well into the twenty-first century and Will was the real cook in our marriage. That was why he did the shopping, so he could choose his own ingredients.

Since then, I had seen Sukie the Sheep (I had to name her) almost daily and Geoff once or twice, usually from a distance but his story made my flesh crawl, probably more as a result of its connection to the house I was now renovating. I always kept an open mind about ghosts and I certainly hoped Matilda was resting in peace, wherever she was.

I surveyed the library. Oak shelving lined the walls. Once these were covered with books but most of them had ended up on one of the many skips we hired to clear out the ruined detritus of many years. The damp and exposure to the elements generally had taken their toll on what must at one time, have been quite a collection of novels and reference and religious books dating back hundreds of years. I wanted to read some but their pages were stuck together, mold and insects had taken over and some were so bad they fell apart as soon as you touched them.

"You could be at this for years and still never get anywhere," Will said as he threw a large bundle into a wheelbarrow ready to transport them outside. They're rotten and they stink to high heaven. Best to get rid of the lot. We can start our own library if you like."

"We won't be staying here that long," I said and didn't like his reaction—a pause, followed by a raised eyebrow before resuming his labors. I stored that up for later. If there was going to be a battle, I wanted time to prepare for it.

The empty room with its high ceiling, plain wooden floor and lack of upholstery meant every movement echoed. I swore even my breath echoed. It was eerie and chilled me. The exercise would warm me up and also take my mind off this inhospitable room. I crossed the floor, trying to ignore the sound of my footsteps, and made my way to the far side where Will and I had stacked the few remaining salvageable books, along with a couple of old tea chests into which I started packing them. An antiquarian bookseller in Leeds had expressed an interest in looking them over, with a view to purchasing them so I wanted to pack them as carefully as possible to avoid any further damage. They were in reasonable condition but still fragile.

I had filled one chest and started on the next. A noise stopped me; a flicker in the corner of my eye. I spun around. It had gone. But, for no more than a second, I was sure I had seen the darting figure of a nun. Maybe the same one I had seen previously.

"Hello?" I called. "Is anyone there?" The silence was almost deafening. My palms were sweating and I rubbed them on my jeans, heedless of the dirt I was transferring. Still nothing. I bent down and lifted more books into the tea chest. I felt something move up behind me. A cold hand touched my bowed head. I froze, incapable of even the slightest movement. I felt whatever was there moving around. I couldn't see it. And I didn't want to. I screwed my eyes tight shut. Even with them closed, I sensed the room grow darker. I smelled dust, fustiness, and something more…a wet animal smell. Musky, unclean. Feral.

Had a dog found its way in? Or a fox? Maybe Sukie or one of the other sheep… At this thought I opened my eyes and the icy feeling evaporated as if it had never been there. The room was as light as it should be for a dull February afternoon. I straightened and looked all around me. There was nothing untoward and no sign of any stray animal. With a sigh I carried on filling the chests until every book was safely packed. I tried not to run out of the room but my pace was hardly a stroll.

I had just finished drying my hands in the kitchen when I heard our car pull up. The Suzuki 4x4 had proved perfect for the poor excuses for roads in the area and Will emerged from it laden with bags of shopping. I greeted him with a kiss at the door.

"I have a treat," he announced a beaming smile lighting up his entire face. "I got a call from the estate agents while I was in the supermarket. Our house is sold. I mean properly sold. The money went into our account this morning and I have now transferred it to the savings accounts we discussed so it will be making us a little money. Isn't that fantastic news?" He swept me off the floor and I tried really hard to swallow my sadness. That was our first house. We had bought it together. Scrimped and saved to make it our home and now strangers would no doubt rip it apart to make it their home. Far from delighted I felt bereft.

He set me down. "What's the matter, Di? You don't look happy. I bought champagne to celebrate," he added, presumably for emphasis or as some sort of hint.

"I know it's good news. Of course it is," I tried. "But I loved that house. I know it was only a little terraced two-bedroom hardly big enough to swing a hamster in, but I shall miss it. That's all."

He took me in his arms. "I know," he said, his voice showing the old tenderness I realized had been missing since we moved up here. "It was very special because it was ours and we had to really work to get it, but it's time to move on. Onwards and upwards thanks to Dad's shrewd investments and Mum's canny thrift. You know, now the money's come through from the sale, I might just invest some of it. Buy some shares. Play the stock market a little. Maybe Dad's magic has worn off on me a bit. Perhaps it's in the genes and all I have to do is tap into it."

I struggled free of his grasp. "Don't get sucked in, Will. Please. People lose everything that way. It's gambling and it can be addictive."

"Don't worry. I'll be careful and I'll take proper advice. From a stockbroker. I've been looking into it and there's a good firm in Leeds. Corinne recommended them."

"Who's Corinne?"

"You remember. Corinne from the estate agency who handled the sale of this house."

"I never met her. You bought this place without my knowledge if you remember."

"I could have sworn... Never mind. I've asked her to dinner on Saturday. She's great company. I'm sure you'll like her and she knows lots of great history about this area. That ruined place that looks like a church—a couple of miles up the road? It's an old abbey called Talamund and it's linked with this place. The stained-glass in the upstairs landing windows came from there and some of the stone in the foundations too. Fascinating. And did you know we have a ghost?"

"Well, after what happened in the library I'm not surprised actually."

"Really?" But I could tell he wasn't listening. "Anyway, she likes to eat most things, has no allergies. I thought a nice traditional roast beef with all the trimmings. She lives alone and you miss out on all that when you're on your own, don't you?"

"I suppose so. Look, how old is this Corinne? Tell me more about her."

"First, I'm opening this champagne. I got it out of the supermarket fridge and it's going to warm up if we don't drink it soon."

He was already twisting the bottle to extract the cork. I reached up into the newly fitted kitchen cupboard and removed two champagne flutes. Maybe the alcohol would calm my nerves which for some reason were becoming increasingly frayed the more he went on. He sounded almost high even though he never touched anything stronger than a few glasses of wine and the occasional Scotch and soda.

The cork popped, followed by a fizzy overload and, amid laughter, he poured the frothing drink into the glasses, set down the bottle and raised his glass. "To us," he said and clinked my glass.

"To us," I replied and sipped my drink. Its refreshing chill tickled my taste buds. I swallowed and sipped more.

"So, what's the rest of her name?"

"Corinne? It's Davenport. She's late twenties, adopted. Birth mother died having her. Father was already dead so she was brought up by two teachers who loved history and instilled that passion in her."

"But she became an estate agent."

"Needed to earn a living I suppose. I mean if you don't want to teach or become an archaeologist there's not a whole lot you can do with a history degree."

"Isn't there? I would have thought the skills you acquire through research, writing and so on would be highly transferable."

"There speaks the careers guidance counsellor."

"Looks like she could have done with some of that. Is she really as passionate about her work as she is about history?"

Will shrugged. "I doubt it. Oh, I forgot, Corinne asked if she could bring Laurence along. He's the stockbroker I mentioned. It'll make a nice foursome and I can pick his brains on the investment front."

"Why not?"

Why not indeed? So why did I feel such a sense of unease, it turned my stomach. I set my glass down. No more champagne for me until I ate something. Will put the shopping away, whistling to himself. It was the first time I had heard him do that since we arrived. In fact, the first time since before his mother died. That should have cheered me but it had the reverse effect. Was Corinne responsible for the smile on his face? He seemed to have found out an awful lot about her. I told myself jealousy was the green-eyed monster that everyone hated, but it wasn't that. I felt an unpleasant clutch of fear. And I had no idea why.

Will had bought pizza and we sat down to eat it, accompanied by a simple salad and the rest of the champagne, now chilling again in an ice bucket. I had debated whether or not to tell Will of my experience that afternoon but decided I would. Maybe talking about it rationally would put it all in perspective. His earlier exuberance had settled into a peacefully happy mood and he listened to me recount the impossible without interrupting. When I finished he set his knife and fork down and leaned back, glass in hand.

"Corinne said this place was probably haunted by its namesake Matilda and the monk who started the abbey. Brother Alfred. This building was completed nearly three hundred years ago but it has the footprint of the original house Matilda built and, as we know, shares some of the original fabric of the abbey as well as the house. Whether you really saw it or not, that could explain the woman and the monk. It was probably just a trick of the light and your mind filled in the blanks, especially given your chat with the farmer."

"Maybe, but you had to be there. It was all so real. It frightened the life out of me."

"It'll be all right once we have the house the way we want it, with our own things around us. It'll be our home then."

Warning bells. "But, Will, we agreed we were going to do this place up and then sell it, move back to your Mum's cottage and decide from there. We were never going to actually make our home here."

"Well, maybe not for long but it doesn't make sense to keep two homes going when we could live here. It's going to take months until we've completed work on all the rooms and those tenants we have are only here for another couple of months and then they're off to their new life in Canada. They've been brilliant. The thought of having to go through the rigmarole of finding new ones for an indeterminate amount of time isn't something I feel like doing if I'm honest."

A wave of anger rose up inside me. "And when were you planning on telling me about this change of plan?"

"It's not really a change of plan."

"Really? I think it most definitely is."

"Corinne thinks it makes sense."

"Oh, Corinne does, does she? Well perhaps you should remember that you're married to me, not Corinne. It's not her opinion that matters it's mine and I don't agree. I'm not living here for one minute after the place is finished and I'm not putting the cottage up for sale. You've already got rid of our first home without my say so, you're not putting me out of that one as well." I pushed my chair back, grabbed my plate and glass and stomped off into the kitchen, leaving a stunned silence behind me.

A few minutes later, I was washing up when Will joined me in the kitchen. He came up behind me and put his hands on my shoulders. I felt his light kiss on my hair.

"You're not getting round me like that," I said and turned my head.

But there was no one there.

My heart found extra beats it didn't know it possessed.

"Will?"

He appeared round the door, empty plate in hand. "Yes?"

My mouth ran dry. "Were you just in here?"

"What?"

"Just now. Did you just come up behind me, put your hands on my shoulders and kiss my hair?"

He didn't need to answer. His look of bewilderment said it all. I reached behind me and gripped the sink with both hands. For a moment, everything seemed to swirl. I blinked rapidly.

"Are you all right. Di? You've gone so pale. Come and sit down."

I let him guide me to a kitchen chair and I sank down, leant forward with my elbows on the small pine table and put my head in my hands.

"God, you're shaking. Whatever's the matter?"

"This bloody house," I said. "There's something wrong here. I want to leave."

Will sat next to me and drew me to him. I leaned into his shoulder, grateful for the tenderness in his caress. It soothed me and I gradually stopped shaking while he stroked my hair.

After a few minutes, he sighed and spoke. "Look, how about this. We'll hold off on the cottage and finish the work here. Then we'll decide. Maybe we could divide our time between the cottage and here when the tenants move out so that it's not left empty for any length of time."

I freed myself and sat up. "Better still, why not simply get tradespeople in to do the work and live at the cottage once the Barratts leave? It's not as if we can't afford it—especially now our other house is sold."

"That will leave this place empty every night. That's how it ended up like this in the first place."

"Then get some security firm in. Rent a couple of guard dogs. I'm telling you, Will, I can't live here. It's playing with my mind. Whether you believe me or not, odd things have happened here today and I haven't felt right about this place since I first laid eyes on it."

Will stared at me. "I can't believe I'm hearing this. You're usually so rational. I never even knew you believed in ghosts."

"I've always kept an open mind. We've never discussed it because there's never been any need to. And that should tell you something. The fact I'm saying these things, behaving like this, you have to see that it's because something is going on that I haven't a clue about. The whole house is off-kilter and it scares the hell out of me. I've never been anywhere that's affected me like this. Never. Not even on a visit to an historic house. And you expect me to live here? No."

"But has anything happened apart from today?"

"Not as such. Not as tangibly, but I keep seeing things out of the corner of my eye and today… Well let's say today something wants me to know it's here and has some sort of plan in mind for me. It touched me, Will. It touched me and then it kissed me."

Will smiled. "A friendly ghost then. Should I be jealous?"

I wanted to slap him. I bit my lip instead. "It's not even remotely amusing, Will. I'm serious. I'm not living here. In fact…" I moved away from the sink and grabbed the hand towel to dry my hands. "You can finish the washing up. I'm going upstairs to pack. I'm going to stay in a hotel tonight."

"What? You can't be serious. How are you even going to get there? We only have one car since we sold yours and you can't leave me stranded out here."

"I'll call a cab."

"Don't be daft. The nearest hotel is miles away. Leeds probably."

He was following me upstairs. I paused and turned on the stair to face him. "And your point is?"

"Why not leave it until the morning. You're angry. My idiotic insensitivity. I'm sorry, Di. I didn't mean to sound so flippant. Sleep on it. See how you feel in the morning. If you're still so sure you can't bear to stay here, I'll drive you."

I paused at the top of the stairs. He was making sense and I was now the one behaving irrationally. What could one more night in this place matter? I'd slept here for weeks already.

But that was before the library. And the kitchen. I pushed those thoughts aside.

"Okay. One more night, But that's it. I'm going to stay in a hotel until the Barratts move out of the cottage. I don't care if I never see this place ever again." I glanced around as I said this, my gaze meeting shadows hiding who knew what secrets? I shuddered at the sudden chill that wrapped itself around me and hugged me in a suffocating embrace. Will kept his gaze steady, watching me, impassively. "Can't you feel anything?" I asked.

"What do you mean? I'm really sorry you feel this way. I am so sure we can make something wonderful out of this place."

"And Corinne agrees with you, does she?" The comment was out before I could stop it and I inwardly cringed at the pettiness of it. This was about so much more than any jealousy I might have for a woman

I had never even laid eyes on, yet I had reduced it to a base level and given Will every excuse to think that some feeling of inadequacy on my part was behind this evening's outburst.

"As a matter of fact she does. I wasn't going to say so, but as you've brought her up again—"

"What is she to you, Will? Really?"

"I don't know what you're implying. At least, I hope I don't."

"Are you having an affair with her?" I don't even know where that came from but it was out now and both of us had to deal with it.

"Don't be ridiculous."

"Since your mother died you've come into a lot of money. She knows that I should imagine?"

"Stop this, Di. Stop it right now. It's crazy and you know it. I have never been unfaithful to you in all the years we've been together. It's never even crossed my mind. Besides, Corinne has a boyfriend. Laurence."

"You seem to know an awful lot about your estate agent."

"She talks a lot and I listen. That's it. The sale was a little complicated at first and we had a few calls and meetings."

"None of which I was party to."

"You were busy at work. All those online conference meetings."

"That didn't stop you telling me what was going on."

"I wanted it to be a surprise. A fantastic, wonderful new venture for us."

"Oh, it was certainly a surprise. More of a shock actually. Have you ever really taken time to get to know this place? I don't mean the room dimensions but the actual atmosphere. It's toxic. There's something really rotten here."

"It's in your head, Diana. You've quit your job. You've got nothing else to focus on except here."

"I quit my job because you insisted on moving. I fully intended to get something up here but so far all my attention has been dragged away to this place."

"Exactly, and that's playing on your mind. You resent this house because of that. You're not giving it a chance. We'll get those builders in to complete the job, then hire decorators. Meanwhile you can look for a job if you want or do some voluntary work since you don't need the money anymore. Whatever you want, Di, but please stop having these crazy thoughts. Promise me."

I could feel the adrenalin subsiding. What Will was saying made perfect sense. Maybe my feelings did stem from resentment at how the house had seemingly been the catalyst for me losing my independence. Maybe he was right. All I needed was something of my own—a job I could get my teeth into the way I always had. There was certainly a void that had opened up the day I reluctantly told my boss I wouldn't be able to continue working for her. We had given it our best shot. She promised me a first-class reference if I needed one and wished me well. I reciprocated. Far worse though was saying goodbye to clients I had worked one to one with for weeks, months and, in some cases, over a year. Most were sanguine about it, wished me well and allowed me to pass them onto one of my colleagues. One though, revealed his true feelings when he angrily told me in a Zoom meeting that I had betrayed him. He accused me of selfishness.

"I trusted you with everything this past eighteen months. I was broken when I came to you for help and you built me up. Now you've destroyed me again. I'll have to start all over and I can't. I'm too old. How *could* you do this to me? How could you?" He cut off the call at that point and blocked me. I told my boss and she tried repeatedly to contact him, without success. Wherever Toby Walters was now I hoped he was all right. Every time I thought of him, I felt a strong wave of guilt. I should have spotted the signs he was becoming too emotionally attached much sooner. The emailed Valentine's card, his tendency to blow a kiss at me as we finished our calls. I had taken this to be in jest, or at the most, a friendly gesture. Looking back, it had been staring me in the face that Toby had unprofessional feelings toward me. And I was flattered, so I let it carry on unabated. He was a good-looking, younger man. Was Will falling into the same trap with Corinne? I would only get a clearer idea by seeing them both together socially. Much as I dreaded it, Saturday evening's dinner would have to proceed. I was glad I wouldn't be cooking it though. I would have struggled to resist the temptation to slip something into her dessert.

Will touched my cheek and the tenderness of the gesture brought tears rushing to my eyes. I touched his hand and interlaced my fingers with his. "Maybe you're right," I said. "Maybe I have let this place take up too much of my time and energy. But I mean it, Will. I don't want to live here."

He smiled. "See how you feel when it's all done up and looking gorgeous. Maybe you'll have a change of heart."

Maybe I would.

But I doubted it.

Chapter Seven

They say you should always sleep on it, and I did. And the following morning, I felt embarrassed by my tirade the previous evening. Neither of us mentioned it. Will didn't say anything about driving me to Leeds and I didn't start packing. With the sun streaming through the window on a glorious sunny morning there didn't seem any point. He had to be right. The atmosphere and legends about this place were playing games with my mind.

Luckily our builder had had a cancellation and could return a couple of days later to do the work we had intended to complete ourselves. Meanwhile we were also knee deep in decorators and paint charts. By Friday, and with no further incidents to report, we had moved on apace. Will left me to go and shop for his dinner party while I showed a decorator round and shared our ideas. Meanwhile Mick, our builder, and his young apprentice, Trevor, along with sundry other contractors, drilled and hammered in various rooms.

By now, we had a viable dining room and living room. The expanded kitchen was fitted with modern units and a central island that Will had always coveted. Our bedroom was comfortable and probably the only room in the house where I felt I didn't have to keep looking over my shoulder. We had managed to salvage an impressive crystal chandelier which had fortunately been covered and, as a result, suffered only minor damage. A further wrought iron one in the hall was already doing its work of providing an impressive welcome as well as shedding light where it should. Despite all the good stuff though, my apprehensions about this house hadn't gone away. I still didn't want to live in it but the need for a fast getaway had receded a little as each successive day brought no fresh disturbances.

Saturday duly arrived and, by six, I had changed into a midi length emerald green dress, trimmed with a broad hem of broderie anglaise, that fitted snugly and served to remind Will that he had always admired my curves. I added uncomfortable, but necessary, stilettos to accentuate my ankles and long legs. Beat that, Corinne!

When the bell rang, Will was basting his roast so I answered the door. One look at Corinne and my mind was transported back to my early teens when I used to watch re-runs of *Desperate Housewives* with my mother. I found the exploits of all the ladies of Wisteria Lane fascinating but now there was only one that leapt to the forefront of my memory. Nicolette Sheridan had portrayed a leggy, predatory, blonde called Edie Britt in whose company no man was safe—whatever their marital status. Corinne could have been her younger self's stand in, right down to the smile which never really left her lips. I felt my heart collapsing in a heap. Nevertheless, I pasted on an equally fake expression.

"You must be Corinne," I said. "I'm Diana. Come in."

She crossed the threshold and only then did I see her companion.

"Laurence," said the man who I gauged to be around thirty. He extended his hand and seemed to appreciate the effort I had gone to. "Pleased to meet you. That dress is gorgeous, isn't it, Corinne?"

"Oh, yes. Lovely," she said, without enthusiasm or even a stray glance in my direction. She was too preoccupied with looking around her.

"Thank you," I said. "Come through. Will's in the kitchen. What can I get you to drink?" My words fell out of my mouth in an untidy heap while I steered my guests into the living room where Corinne made straight for the sofa. She sat, crossing her slim, fake-tanned legs.

"Vodka with tonic and ice please," she said.

Laurence joined her. "Scotch for me please, with ice and a little water."

Anger began to coil its way up into my throat—mostly directed at myself. I tried to steady my shaking fingers as they fumbled with the catch on the drinks cabinet, frustrated at why my usually well-coordinated digits seemed hellbent on fighting against me. As far as I was aware, Corinne had done nothing to me except exist. Well, that and the fact she was clearly far more self-assured than I was. Finally, the catch slipped open. I bit my lip and reached for the bottles and glasses. As if on cue, Will appeared with our ice bucket.

"I see you've introduced yourselves," he said, handing me the ice.

"We have indeed," I said, knowing my tone fell somewhere between brusque and uncomfortable. "Scotch?" The questioning look in his eyes as I asked this told me he was only too aware that I was off-kilter, to say the least.

"Oh, er, yes, please," he said. Evidently, my discomfiture was infectious. An awkward silence would have ensued had Laurence not spoken up and made some comment about nice smells wafting in from the kitchen.

I handed Corinne her drink and noticed the immaculately manicured nails as she accepted the glass from me. I knew mine did not shape up. I was too engaged in house renovation to worry about acrylics and nail polish. Still, now we had people in to do that for us, maybe I would treat myself to a pamper day. My hair could do with a good trim too and my roots needed attention.

After two drinks Corinne stretched, cat-like, and leaned back, almost as if she was taking ownership of the sofa. Any moment and she would start purring. My animosity towards her grew with every passing moment, but her boyfriend was another matter. Laurence was quite charming. I liked the way his eyes crinkled up when he smiled. He made me feel appreciated. Somehow, since leaving my job, I hadn't experienced a lot of that. Will was too preoccupied to even notice me. I knew it shouldn't matter and I was being far too precious but, still, Laurence's smiles and apparent willingness to give anything I said some consideration contrasted sharply with Will's reaction to me. He seemed far more intent on listening to Corinne. He was practically hanging on her every word. I told myself I was being stupid and it seemed to work because, after two glasses of a decent Chablis, I even managed to put my feelings for her aside, at least a shade, as I started to feel nicely mellow. So much so that I had to remind myself I hadn't eaten anything all day. I set my glass down. Nothing more until after the first course.

Laurence instigated most of the conversation. He was an information gatherer, wanting to know everything about everything, including me. As time ticked by and the roast neared completion, Will disappeared from time to time to attend to the various stages of our meal, which left me holding the fort and mainly talking to him. Corinne mostly sipped her drink and stared into space. I left her there. Laurence seemed surprised I hadn't met her before.

"Will wanted to surprise me with this house," I said. "And he certainly did that."

"I can imagine," Laurence said, laughing. He had a pleasant laugh, warm and kind of sexy. I told myself to stop thinking about that and decided no more wine until well into the main course.

Corinne chose that moment to join the conversation, directing her comments to Laurence. "That was probably my fault," she said. "I convinced Will that she would probably have a fit if she saw this house in its dilapidated state and that it would be far better to wait until he had renovated it and then present her with the keys. He agreed initially, the sale went through but then he got cold feet. He said it wouldn't be fair to renovate without Diana being involved in the decisions so he jumped the gun. I should imagine it came as quite a shock." Again the fake smile.

Emboldened by the alcohol, I decided to give as good as I got. "Oh, I wouldn't say that. Surprise yes. But what a lovely thing for him to do. Not every woman is given a house she can have carte blanche on. I'm having the time of my life deciding what décor to have and what room themes to choose."

"I'm sure," Laurence said.

Corinne resumed her communion with space and I mentally chalked up my tiny victory.

The meal itself was delicious and the conversation gradually relaxed more as the evening progressed. By the time we reached the coffee and liqueurs, even Corinne's smile had become more natural.

Will and Laurence seemed to be hitting it off well and I did my best to keep my contributions flowing but even though I tried, Corinne increasingly rattled me. There was nothing concrete I could pin down, just something about her seemed off somehow. More than once I caught her when she thought no one's attention was on her and it was then I realized. She wasn't merely staring off vaguely. In this room at least, she was actually staring *fixedly* at a point somewhere off to the far end of the room. Without turning round and making it obvious, I couldn't follow her line of sight but when the opportunity presented itself in the form of a need to replenish everyone's drinks, I stood and circulated around the table in order to pour out the after-dinner brandy. As I stood behind her, I stole a glance in the direction that had so captivated her. There was nothing there. Just the blank wall. It needed a picture or mirror or something because it was noticeably bare, but was that any reason to give it so much attention?

Baffled I moved back to my seat, taking care to replace the bottle out of reach on the sideboard in case I needed another excuse to shift my focus.

We adjourned back into the living room for more drinks. Will was back on his Scotch, heavily drowned in soda, while I stuck to wine. As designated driver, Laurence was abstaining and stuck to coffee while Corinne nursed a cognac, swirling it before each sip. She had crossed those perfectly tanned legs of hers and the skirt had ridden up high. It was proving quite fascinating for Will who didn't seem to be able to take his eyes off her. From her expression I knew she had noticed and was enjoying the attention. Anger rose inside me and I swallowed hard.

By now it was after ten, still early but I was looking for ways I could draw this uncomfortable evening to a close. Not easy, when everyone else seemed to be really enjoying themselves while the effort of pasting a smile on my face was making my jaws ache.

The conversation had moved on from local gossip and assorted trivia to favorite vacation resorts. Corinne held out her glass for Will to top up as he brought the Courvoisier to her. One spaghetti strap of her dress slipped down her free arm. It didn't reveal anything, but the action in itself was sexually charged. At the same time, she shifted position so that her dress rode up even higher. A couple more inches and we would be able to tell what color her underwear was—if she was even wearing any. Seething with suppressed rage, I looked across at Laurence who seemed totally unperturbed. Surely he could see what was happening. He was right opposite her. Will also didn't visibly react. If I said anything now, I would look like a jealous, insecure wife complaining about nothing, but if I stayed any longer in that room, I wouldn't be able to hold in my anger. I stood. The conversation kept on flowing so I took myself out of the room and into the kitchen where I proceeded to run hot water for the washing up.

Ten minutes in and I heard footsteps approaching along the stone-flagged hallway.

Laurence appeared round the open door. He was smiling. "Want some help?"

Someone had actually noticed my departure. Tears rushed to my eyes and I hurriedly looked down at the bowl so he wouldn't see. He came up close behind me and picked up a tea towel.

"Don't worry about Corinne," he said. "She's always like that. She's not really aware of what she's doing."

"Oh, you believe that, do you?" I couldn't keep the cutting edge out of my voice, He set the towel down and touched my wet hand.

"Hey, look at me."

I raised my eyes and prayed the tears away. But one slipped out and he caught it with his finger. "She's too full-on. I've told her before but she doesn't realize the impact she has. She's not predatory you know. Not really."

Maybe I should have been reassured but I wasn't. Especially when he stroked my cheek and leaned in to give me a light peck. I moved back and he picked up the towel again.

"I'm sorry," he said. "I thought you might need a little comforting. You looked so…lost for a moment."

Had I misjudged him? His smile was warm and genuine enough but…then I remembered.

"You've left them alone in there."

"Yes. Don't worry, they're adults. They're not going to play with matches and set the house ablaze or anything."

"It's not that kind of fire I'm worried about." I threw the dishcloth into the sink sending splashes of bubbly hot water flying. I charged out, down the hall and into the living room where my husband and his estate agent sat almost as I had left them. Corinne had adjusted her dress and had even pulled the skirt down to a more acceptable length. At my hurried entrance, they both stared at me.

My heart was thumping, my dripping hands had nowhere to hide and I certainly couldn't wipe them on my dress which, I noticed with dismay, was speckled with splashes from the water. They would dry and disappear but right now my beautiful emerald dress looked as if I had been caught in a rainstorm.

"Is everything all right, Di?" Will asked as he came over to me and steered me to my chair. "Yes, yes, fine. Laurence was helping me with the washing up and I suddenly realized what a lousy hostess I was being, leaving my guests. Sorry. Does anyone want another drink?"

Corinne glanced at her watch and set her empty glass down. "Not for me thanks, I think we should be setting off now. Work tomorrow. First appointment at nine-thirty. Thank you for a lovely evening. The meal was excellent and you have been a charming hostess, Di."

An inward cringe and my hands clenched at my sides. I forced yet another fake smile on my face to acknowledge her thanks. But she had crossed a line. No one but Will called me Di. Ever.

Laurence took me briefly to one side as Corinne retrieved her bag from the dining room. "I'm sorry if I overstepped the mark in the kitchen. No harm done I hope?"

"No, of course not. Just me being silly. I'm not usually like that. This house..."

"Oh yes, this house. Ask Will what Corinne was telling him about when I came to join you. I've heard the stories before but I don't think you have."

Corinne was back. Will in tow. "Hope to see you again soon, Di. It was really nice to meet you. Will has told me so much about you and it was great to be able to put it all into context."

"Nice to meet you too, Corinne," I said, and hoped my clenched teeth didn't betray me.

I closed the door, locked and bolted it, venting my spleen on shoving the bolt particularly hard so it rattled.

"Wow, you meant that, didn't you?" Will laughed. "Come on, let's get that washing up finished and you can tell me what's been bothering you."

"Oh, you noticed, did you? You seemed a little preoccupied."

Will paused before she let out a nervous laugh. "You can't be serious. Is this *jealousy*? You're jealous of Corinne? Why, for heaven's sake?"

"Oh, let me see. Maybe the ever-shrinking skirt and forward thrust of her not inconsiderable cleavage for starters."

"Don't be ridiculous, Di."

"And who told her she could call me Di? Apart from you, I am Diana to everyone who doesn't call me Mrs. Clarke."

"She's heard me refer to you as Di and picked it up from there. Perfectly innocent. I'll tell her not to in future."

"I see no reason why there should be any future. The sale is complete. We have no more business to conduct with her."

"Except she is Laurence's girlfriend and he's my stockbroker."

"Not yet and even if he was, we don't have to see them socially."

"And what if I want to see them socially. I happen to like Laurence and we don't have any friends up here yet."

"Then we'll make new friends. We'll join something. You can take up golf."

Will laughed. "Golf! Bloody hell, Di. How old do you think I am? I'd die of boredom and so would you, or are you planning on becoming a golf widow in this indeterminate future you seem to have mapped out for us?"

"Now who's being ridiculous?"

"What exactly is your problem with Corinne? You surely don't think there's anything going on between us?"

"Well, is there?"

"How the hell can you say that? I'm married to the woman I love. I don't fool around. End of."

I ran out of steam. Was Will right? We had been together since high school. He had never strayed before. I was as certain as I could be about that. I shook my head and marched into the kitchen to resume clearing up, Will followed me.

He took over where Laurence had left off, drying up dishes. "While you were out earlier, Corinne told me something about the history of this place. I know we have the stuff about Matilda, the renegade Welsh monk and the abbey up the road, but more recently there's been a bit of a checkered history."

"Oh?" I tried to sound more interested than I was. Inside my stomach was churning as my emotions crashed and clashed their way through my body.

"You know I told you the previous owners died? Well, that's true but there's a lot more to the story. Those owners bought it for a song at an auction around twenty years ago. Apparently they intended to do what we're doing but it never happened. Back then quite a lot of work had been done on the place but there was still plenty to do. The couple moved up here from the Channel Islands. Guernsey, Corinne thinks. Newly married and full of ideas along with the money to see them through, but just a few weeks after they arrived something happened that blew their whole relationship apart. They split up but what took place right after that is a mystery. He—Mr. Le Pellier I think his name was?"

"That's right, Christian Le Pellier. Her name was Jacqueline. I saw it on the documents Corinne gave you."

"That's it. He came home one day and found his wife in bed with some mystery man. Naturally he blew his top and she calmly informed him she was pregnant with this man's child and had no further use for her husband."

"Who reported that then? The aggrieved husband?"

"Yes, by way of a letter to his mother in Guernsey. He then disappeared for six weeks during which time his mother and sister, out of their minds with worry, reported him missing, flew up here and mounted a search. It was in the papers, on the news and then, this is where it gets like Agatha Christie. You know how *she* disappeared from her home in Devon and didn't turn up for ten days. Then someone spotted her at a hotel in Harrogate where she was staying under the name of her then-husband's mistress?"

"There's an old film about it. Dustin Hoffmann played a reporter. I can't remember who played Agatha. Vanessa Redgrave, maybe?—"

"Yes, but never mind that. A few people came forward and said they'd seen Christian working on a farm in Scotland. Somewhere near Dumfries. There was a tearful reunion with his mother. He'd apparently suffered some sort of breakdown over the business with his wife. He went back to Guernsey to live, but the odd thing is he never sold the house. It remained in his and his wife's name. She was never seen again and is presumed to have run off with this man whose identity has never been established. Christian Le Pellier died a year ago, of natural causes. Corinne isn't sure of the exact circumstances."

"So that's when his family put the house on the market?"

"Yes. Corinne met Le Pellier's brother, Patrick. By all accounts he couldn't wait to get back to Guernsey. Told her to sell the house as fast as possible to the first buyer who came along."

"So that's how you got it at a knock-down price?"

"Don't judge me," Will said, and laughed. "Seriously, it was a fair price all things considered. Less than what they were asking but Corinne told me afterwards that she had bumped it up a bit to give her some wiggle room. What I offered was what Patrick had said he would be happy with anyway."

"Which actually means you could have probably got it for less but, as you say, it was a fair price and no one can feel they've been cheated."

"Thanks, Di. I'm glad you feel like that because that's the way I feel too."

What can I say? It was only when I woke up feeling warm and fuzzy the following morning that I realized we had made love in that house for the first time that night.

Chapter Eight

The following weeks saw constant activity in the house. The workmen made huge inroads, sorting out areas of dry rot, fitting new floorboards to the accompaniment of endless, brain-jarring sawing, hammering and drilling. My desire for an en suite bathroom for what we had adopted as the master bedroom turned into a more major project than it had first appeared, thanks to the vagaries of the outdated plumbing. More workmen arrived to sort it out, adding their noise and mess to the echoing halls. The vibrations set the crystal in the bedroom chandelier tinkling. It was a timeless, almost cheerful sound which felt at odds with the rest of the house.

I still had problems even entering the library. In contrast to the increasingly open and light environment we were creating elsewhere, this room oozed darkness and an ominous atmosphere that I found oppressive. I didn't like to spend any time in there alone and one morning, while Will was occupied with an assessment of the outbuildings, I collared Mick to accompany me. He brought Trevor along—a shy young lad who looked less than his probable age of sixteen.

"What do you reckon about us removing all the bookcases in here?" I asked him.

He made that curious sucking noise people in his profession have down to a fine art and which almost always precedes the announcement that you will need to sacrifice your entire savings and then some. He said nothing, but chose instead to make a tour of the room, systematically inspecting the walls and the bookcases themselves. Inspection complete, he took out his phone and tapped rapidly for a few seconds. He then joined me in the center of the room. "Actually, it's probably not as much as I first thought. Depends on what you're looking for of course and what we find when we get those bookcases down. The wood's rotten and they've been there a couple of centuries but, all in all, we could be looking at…" He passed his phone to me.

I blinked. I had anticipated a figure that was a few thousand more than this but concentrated on keeping my expression blank. I handed the phone back. "Is that your best offer?" I asked, adding a smile to my face which I hoped would encourage him.

"Well, like I say, depends on what we find under there, but it may be a little less. Not significantly though. And I am bearing in mind all the other work you've given us. That's really my best estimate."

"Very well. I'll talk to Will and we'll get back to you."

"Great. I could carry on with it when we've finished upstairs but best be quick because I could get a call anytime offering me another big job."

"I'll speak to him over lunch and let you know what he says."

"Are you sure you want to get rid of those lovely bookcases, Di? They add such character to the place. A proper library."

"There's nothing to stop someone having a proper library, just not with those shelves. Mick said the wood's rotten. It's a wonder they didn't come down of their own accord with the weight of all those books on them."

Will chewed on his roast beef sandwich in silence. Then, "Do you want to get another quote first?"

"I don't see the point. Mick's a good builder and we know the quality of his work. His brother does all the joinery. Besides if we went elsewhere for that job it could cause bad feeling and the last thing we need is an unhappy builder. He's still got the landings to finish."

Will nodded. "Okay. So what do you want in place of those bookcases then?"

"I thought just walls for now with our freestanding bookcases. It'll open the room up and make it less claustrophobic. Soft gray walls perhaps. Maybe a feature darker wall."

Will stood and took his plate to the sink. "I'll leave it to you. You're the one with good taste. I'd just mess it up."

"I'll tell Mick now. Oh, how are the outbuildings coming on? Found anything interesting?"

There was a clatter from the sink. "Sorry, just dropped my plate. A couple of curiosities. I'll show you later when I've gone through everything. Most is just general detritus. Stuff destined to be taken to a rubbish tip that somehow never made it that far. There's old newspapers from the 1930s. Hitler's annexation of Poland, that sort of thing. There's an interesting box. It's locked and I can't see a key yet but I'll bring it in and we'll see if we can get into it. I can always force it if necessary."

"I love old boxes. You never know what you're going to find in them."

Will set aside the tea towel he had used to dry up our plates. He put his arms loosely around me and planted a soft kiss on my forehead. "You're going to love this old house one day," he said. "I'm sure of it."

I was equally certain I wasn't. I watched as he left me in the kitchen and a curious feeling of loneliness swept over me.

Mick was delighted and produced paint charts. He suggested I might consider wallpaper but if the room was destined to be still some sort of library it seemed a waste.

Three weeks later, Mick and Trevor turned their attention to demolition. Two skips sat in our yard, awaiting the wood. They were rapidly being filled when Mick called me in.

"We've found something we don't think you were aware of," he said. "Certainly surprised us."

I followed him into the devastated room. Three walls were stripped of their floor-to-ceiling bookcases. The walls underneath showed signs of black mold and the smell was damp, fusty, unpleasant. "Best to wear a mask in here," Mick said, handing me one. "Those spores from that mold aren't healthy. I'm bringing a mate of mine in. He's got all the stuff to get rid of that." He gestured at the black-speckled walls before putting on his mask.

I donned the mask and followed Mick to the back of the room where Trevor was waiting, similarly attired. At first I didn't see it but then…

In the wall was a keyhole. There was no handle and the outline of a door was only visible if you looked closely. This wall was devoid of black mold and seemed somehow more modern than the rest. I told Mick so.

"And you're right. That's because this is a later wall. This room should be a good few inches longer but at some stage, someone has decided to chop off those inches or maybe more than just a few inches. I think there's another room through there or at the least an entrance to something."

Hairs rose on the back of my neck. "When do you think they did that? I mean those bookcases have been here for a couple of hundred years or more haven't they?"

"That's the interesting thing. When we started on this wall we realized at once that it wasn't like the others. Nowhere near as old. I couldn't tell you how old exactly but they've done a good job. Whoever built the bookcases here wanted them to blend in completely. You'll have noticed that this is the only wall that's not damp. And the plastering is definitely not pre-early twentieth century. All you need now is to find the key to whatever lies behind that door."

"Or you could simply take the wall down. You said it was a later addition so presumably it wouldn't affect the integrity of the building."

"True, but do you really want to get rid of it? This isn't some plasterboard, botched job. It's a proper wall. Wouldn't it be an idea to find out what's there first? You might want to keep your secret room."

He had a point. Besides, I had no intention of living here so whoever bought it from us might have their own reasons for wanting it as it was. "Okay, let's leave it alone then. I'll get a locksmith because unless Will has found anything outside, I'm pretty certain we don't have the key."

I left them to carry on and went in search of Will. The outbuildings were across the yard. At one time they had probably housed animals, maybe sheep or even a horse. There was also the remains of an outside toilet that was destined to be demolished. I found my husband in the larger of the two other adjoining buildings. Despite the sunshine outside, it was dark and depressing in that place with its millstone grit walls.

He didn't notice me at first, so absorbed was he in whatever he was inspecting. He jumped when I coughed.

"God, Di, you scared the life out of me. It's so quiet in here. I didn't expect you. Something happened?"

"Mick's found a secret hideaway in the library. There's a wall that's been built much later than the rest with a locked door for which I'm assuming we don't have a key so we'll need a locksmith again but…come on and see for yourself."

Mick dropped the book he had been studying so intently and we made our way to the library, "You'll need a mask. It's pretty vile in there."

Masked up, and with only his eyes visible, it was impossible to tell Will's true reaction to the discovery. He stared at it and said nothing for a few moments. Mick said nothing while his apprentice shifted his weight from one foot to another and stared down at his plaster-coated fingers.

"Well, what do you make of that?" I said at last.

"I…don't really know what to make of it. A priest's hole?"

"Nah," Mick said, "Too late on for that. That's sixteenth century. This house wasn't even built at that time and this has been done later than that; no more than a hundred or so years ago, if that."

"I told Mick we need a locksmith to open it," I said. "Who knows what's on the other side?"

"Perhaps we're better off not knowing," Will said.

Had he taken leave of his senses? "You can't be serious."

"Look at the evidence. It's been blocked off by someone who clearly thought its secrets were best kept hidden. So well hidden they built an entire wall so that it would never be found."

"But it *has* been found. By us. We can't just paint over it and pretend it's not there. Besides, we need a key and there isn't one, is there?"

Will shook his head.

I persisted, "You can't sell a property with a locked room with no key."

"I'm sure it happens all the time with historic houses."

"This wouldn't be sold as a historic house. People want to get into the rooms in their houses. And anyway, there might be valuable stuff in there."

"Buried treasure you mean?" Will laughed, but not a pleasant sound.

Mick was watching the exchange, frowning. I began to feel embarrassed. What was the matter with my husband?

"Well," I said, "Tomorrow morning I'm going to find a locksmith and get them to come out once the room's cleared and the mold's dealt with, but before the redecorating starts."

"Do what you like," Will said and left.

I stared after him. "Sorry about that, Mick. I don't know what's the matter with him."

"Don't worry, Mrs. Clarke. Probably preoccupied with all the work going on here."

"Probably," I agreed, but I knew that wasn't it.

Chapter Nine

A sleepless night left me certain I could not wait until the room was cleared before finding out what lay behind that locked door. For it to have been hidden like that screamed of it being something important. I didn't tell Will of my intentions. He clearly wasn't keen on the idea but if he came home and found it done, there was nothing he could do about it.

I phoned three locksmiths before I found one who agreed to come out that same afternoon. Will was in Leeds seeing Laurence to talk about investments. He seemed a little surprised, and definitely relieved when I said I would stay behind. Thankfully he didn't press me when I gave some vague excuse about wanting to sort a few things out. Of course that was another sign things weren't right between us. Normally Will would have sensed something was afoot and questioned me on it. But then, normally there would have been no need for any subterfuge. I would have come straight out and told him what I intended to do.

Mick and his apprentice were busy working on the mountain of debris that had accumulated on the floor of the library when I brought the locksmith in. Both he and I were not only masked but also suitably garbed in protective coveralls.

"Is that you Derek?" Mick asked, "Difficult to tell with that mask on."

"Aye, it's me, Mick. What have we here then?"

"Secret door by the looks of it. Old Matilda and her monk up to naughty tricks no doubt. Had to have somewhere to do it away from prying eyes I expect."

"Oh no, that can't be right, can it?" I said. "I mean this building is much later than the one she lived in."

"True enough," Mick said. "Most of it certainly. But I've had a think about that since we first found it. This side of the house has some of the original building left in it. Not just the stones from the demolished earlier structure but the actual wall and possibly a bit more besides. So maybe…. Not sure really. I've never examined it that closely from the outside. *This* wall's much later, as I said to you. I reckon pre-Second World War but maybe not as early as the First—but that's not to say it didn't replace an earlier one."

"Old man Dempster lived here in the first half of the last century didn't he? Him with all them daughters of his. Or were they?" He gave a knowing laugh, echoed by Mick.

"Dempster?" I asked. "I've not heard of him."

"Oh, he was a rum one," Mick said and Derek nodded. "He lived here for years. Dressed in black robes. Not like a monk though. These had symbols on them. Moons and stars and such like. My gran said there were young women living here. They came and went but he always called them his daughters. Not that he had much to do with anyone really, and the girls even less. They just wandered around, dressed in flowing dresses like nymphs."

"Nymphs?"

"Yes," both men said together.

"They were always dancing around bonfires on warm summer nights. Sometimes on Halloween too. Gran said her mother used to keep the kids in."

"Everyone's mam did," Derek said. "Proper weird lot."

"What happened to them?"

Mick and Derek exchanged looks and both shrugged.

Derek shifted his weight. "One day, people realized they hadn't seen any sign of life for weeks and the local policeman was sent up to check on them. The place was empty but there had been signs of some building work done inside. Maybe that's when this went up," he pointed to the wall.

"Aye," Mick agreed. "That would be in the early 1930s. It fits. The place lay empty for years until that couple bought it back in the mid-1990s. Can't remember their names and they weren't there long when both of them died in accidents. Their friends bought it straightaway after that. Peter and Lynn Schofield. Never got to know them. Lots of deaths around then. The last one was Peter Schofield. His wife ran him over. Accident as far as they could tell but it sent her over the edge. She was pregnant too. He survived the accident but was pretty much housebound so they had regular visits by the social services because of her condition and mental state. She would ramble on about how she was possessed and her husband was old Brother Alfred who had got her pregnant. Oh, a real rum do that was. There was talk of what would happen to the baby when it was born because neither of them was in any fit state to look after it. But none of them lived to tell the tale. She had the baby, killed her husband and then herself. Horrible business. That's how come the Le Pelliers came to live here." Mick and Derek exchanged raised eyebrows and shook their heads.

"What happened to the baby?" I asked. "After the woman killed her husband and herself. Did it survive?"

Mick and Derek exchanged another glance.

"I can't recall, can you. Derek?" Mick asked.

Derek shrugged. "Dunno. Can't remember anyone mentioning it. Of course we were only kids at the time. I expect Social Services took it and it got adopted. That's what usually happens isn't it?"

"I expect you're right. How awful though."

"There's all sorts of stories about the original inhabitants of this place and the old abbey," Derek said. "When you grow up around here they're as much a part of your life as any fairy tale and with probably about as much truth in them too."

It seemed the more you dug, the deeper the pit of misery that surrounded Matilda's Retreat. No wonder it held such a dark atmosphere. But there was clearly more. Maybe a great deal more, and I needed to know as much as possible if I was to finally convince Will of the folly of remaining here. "What sort of stories?" I asked. "I mean, apart from what you've just told me—and what happened with the Le Pelliers. What about the earlier inhabitants? What went on there?"

"Devil worship for one thing," Derek said. "Caught up with them in the end though. Matilda and Brother Alfred were both burned as witches. The story goes they used to sacrifice in the house here and up at the abbey. Nuns mainly. Young ones. Virgins you see. Sacrificed to the devil. And babies when they could get hold of them, but I think Brother Alfred preferred the nuns. They were more to his taste."

"Now, now, Derek, ladies present."

"Oh don't mind me," I said, as lightheartedly as I could manage with a cold shiver running down my spine. I didn't want them to stop now. "What else do you know?"

Mick rolled his eyes. Derek was clearly warming to his subject. "Matilda was besotted with Brother Alfred. That wasn't his real name though. He was Welsh."

"Oh, I know that bit. Afagddu ap Llewellyn."

"That's the fellow. Bit of a mouthful. Not surprised they changed it. Anyway she gave him all her money and became his willing slave. There wasn't a thing she wouldn't do for him. She would even kill for him. She butchered those nuns. They said blood dripped off the walls by the time she finished."

"Derek. That's going a bit far," Mick said.

"I'm only telling Mrs. Clarke what we all heard growing up."

"And I'm quite sure there has been a lot of adding to over the years. Don't worry, Mrs. Clarke. It was probably pretty awful but not as bad as Derek's making out. But it's those legends that will have attracted the likes of Dempster."

"They've found a lot of bones up at the abbey," Derek said. "Human bones. Over a period of time that is. Soil erosion. Years of heavy storms wash away the topsoil and every so often they come across random bones. Never a whole body, you understand, just parts, as if they've been chopped up and buried. My granddad told me the first time he remembers someone's dog digging up a femur. Not twelve feet from the back wall of the abbey. Police thought at first there'd been a recent murder but some scientist at the university in Leeds said it was too old for that."

The shiver was affecting my whole body now. "So they were sacrificing people up at the abbey, but also here? In the old house?"

Derek and Mick nodded. "That's what the stories say," Mick said.

"That's why I'm here so quickly," Derek added. "This place has always intrigued me. When you called and said your builder had discovered an old door with no key in this place, curiosity got the better of me. I'm afraid there's a lady in Wainstalls that's going to have to wait another day for her window locks."

I wanted to hear more but was conscious of the time. Will said he would be back around five and it was already half past three. "You'd best get started then," I said.

"Certainly will. Cup of tea wouldn't come amiss though. Strong, dash of milk, three sugars please."

I glanced at Mick who nodded and over at Trevor, the apprentice, who had paused in his sweeping up, the better to hear the sordid details of the long-ago owners of this house.

When I returned, Derek had already forced the lock. "Thought I'd hang on until you got here before I opened it," he said.

I laid down the tray with their teas and joined them. Without a handle, opening the door was no easy matter but successive assaults with a variety of tools in both Derek's and Mick's collections and the wooden door finally gave up and allowed itself to be wrenched open with a lot of protesting creaks.

Plaster came away from the wall and crumbled into dust. We had a certificate assuring us there was no asbestos in the building and I sincerely hoped that extended to this part. The fact that neither of the two professionals seemed concerned enough to mention it was reassuring.

The door was a couple of inches open and with all three of the men tugging at it, more plaster came away and then, with a loud crack, the door fell off its hinges. A sudden rush of foul air sent us reeling.

I coughed and spluttered. Derek, Mick and Trevor rested the door against the wall before retreating in a mass of coughing. Beyond where the door had stood, a black hole greeted us. I rushed to the other side of the room to open the windows as wide as possible, stuck my head out of the window and removed my mask to take in lungfuls of sweet fresh air.

The three men joined me and we all leaned out of the large picture windows.

"You'll need to keep these open for a day or two I reckon," Mick said.

I had already determined that so I merely nodded. "What do you reckon is behind there?" I asked.

Mick shrugged. "From what I could see, it's a narrow passageway. Probably no longer than the length of that wall. But it's no more than two-foot-six wide. We'll need some lighting to see for sure. Have you got any flashlights? I have but not here."

"There's one in the kitchen. I'll get it."

By the time I returned, the men were drinking their tea and discussing the hole in the wall. The smell didn't seem as bad now, unpleasant rather than unbearable.

The flashlight was the large, handheld variety with a powerful beam. When Mick switched it on it illuminated a stone wall. "That's your exterior. I reckon that's your original wall from the old building." He shone it down onto the floor which seemed to consist of dried mud. Mick tested it with his foot. "Yeah. That's the ground all right. Odd thing to do but then this is not your average house, is it?" He flashed the light to the right. "Doesn't go far. Not even to the end of this room. It's blocked off with stone." He flashed upward. "Looks like that goes right up. That would explain why I never noticed anything peculiar when we were up in the attic."

He flashed the beam to the left. "Ah, right, here we go. The floor disappears. About three or four feet in.... There's steps leading down. Beyond the stairwell, it's blocked off again."

"Let me see," I said. Mick handed me the flashlight.

"Be careful now. Don't be going in there. You could easily fall down and we don't know how deep it is."

I didn't need telling but nodded anyway. I held onto what remained of the door frame and put one foot over the threshold, enough to be able to see what Mick had just seen. Sure enough, there was the beginning of a series of steps, with no banister to hang onto.

After a moment or two to absorb what I was looking at, I withdrew and switched off the flashlight. "It's like whoever built the new house wanted to preserve this and built around it."

"That's what it looks like," Mick said and Derek nodded. "He took the windows from the abbey, and some of the stone so they say. Maybe he had a soft spot for the old bugger. Brother Alfred I mean."

"Maybe he was part of the same sect," I said.

"Oh no!" Trevor startled me. I had never heard him do more than mumble his thanks for the endless mugs of tea I made.

"Now then, young Trevor," Mick said, laying a hand on the lad's arm. "Don't worry yourself."

But it was too late for that. "I'm sorry, Uncle Mick. Me Mam told me no good would come of me working here. She's been at me and at me and this place is so weird. I told you what happened yesterday—"

"Trevor!" Mick's admonishment shut him up and he cast his tear-filled eyes downward.

"What happened yesterday?" I asked. Trevor looked up.

"Now, don't worry about Trevor, Mrs. Clarke. He's not…well, how can I put it these days? He didn't do very well at school. Not academic. Had trouble with his reading and writing and learning stuff."

But I wasn't going to let this drop. "Something happened, didn't it, Trevor?"

Mick intervened again. "It were nowt. Nothing to get het up about. The boy thought he saw something but I explained he couldn't have and that was that."

"What was it you think you saw, Trevor? No please, Mick I would like him to answer for himself because I've also seen a couple of things I couldn't explain."

"Very well, Mrs. Clarke if you say so. Trevor, tell the lady."

"She were a nun. Not a nice one like in *The Sound of Music*. She looked angry." He seemed about to say more but shook his head and looked down at his feet again.

"See? He saw something out of the corner of his eye, that's all. We've all done it. The sun coming out from the cloud. Shadows in the room. Nothing to worry about. He's very imaginative is our Trevor. He's my sister's youngest. The other two are at university. You wouldn't believe it would you? She reckoned her eggs were old and the one that worked was defective. She didn't have him till she was over forty." He and Derek laughed.

I cringed. If poor Trevor had this to contend with at home it was little wonder he rarely spoke up for himself. I vowed to get him on his own. The next day would do. I could ask him to help me with some small task in the kitchen and, while he was doing that, work on getting him to open up about whatever it was he had really seen.

It could have been worse. Will didn't even seem angry. "I've just seen Mick getting into his van with that boy of his. He said he hoped I enjoyed exploring down the rabbit hole. Something about a hole in the library wall? What have you been up to, Di?"

"I phoned a locksmith. Curiosity got the better of me. I'm sorry for not mentioning it to you first but I seized the moment and…. Come and see for yourself. It's fascinating. A bit smelly but fascinating."

Will took the mask and overalls from me and secured it in place as we made our way into the library. Perhaps I was just used to it by now but the smell didn't seem too bad. Will, on the other hand…

"Oh my God. Where's that stench coming from? Did something die through there?"

"It hasn't been opened in decades. It's just stale air," I hoped. "Here." I handed him the flashlight. "Switch that on and have a peek. Take care though because there's a staircase right there and I don't know how steep it is or where it leads."

Will stood at the doorway and flashed the beam around. "What is it? Some kind of priest's hole?"

"Doesn't fit with the known history of this place. It seems it's part of the original building and was preserved for some reason by the man who built this one and at least one subsequent owner—the one who erected this later wall. Why they did that is a different matter."

Will stepped inside.

"Be careful where you step. Can you see the stairs now?"

I could see the light dancing on the walls and then it moved away. Will's voice echoed off the walls. "It's dark as hell down there but the steps are solid enough. Made of the same stone as the exterior walls. A bit uneven. There's no handrail but you can steady yourself with the wall. I'm going down there, Di."

"Do you think you should? Don't you need more light?"

His voice was growing a little fainter, telling me he had already commenced his descent.

"It's okay Di. I'm at the bottom. Can you still hear me?"

"You sound quite far away but I can. What's it like down there?"

"Nothing much to see…oh, hang on a minute. Bloody hell!"

"What is it? What's down there?"

"It's a small room. No light. There's…chains." I heard a jangling. "Oh God, Di. They used to keep people down here. These are manacles. They chained people to the floor."

I felt sick. "Leave it, Will. Leave it. We'll get it bricked up."

His voice was growing fainter as he spoke, "There's more. Hang on. There's some kind of…. It looks like a kind of altar you'd have in a church and there's something hanging on the wall." He went quiet.

The silence scared me. "Will, what is it? Speak to me."

Silence. "Will, for God's sake, you're scaring me. *Will!*"

The beam bounced off the walls. Will's face was ashen as he emerged from the dark up the steps.

"Tell me, Will, what happened?"

In the light of the library, he shook off the dust and cobwebs that had attached themselves to him. His hands were shaking. He set down the flashlight. Meanwhile my heart was beating so fast I thought I would have some kind of cardiac arrest while Will was clearly having trouble ordering his thoughts.

"It was really bad down there, wasn't it?" I asked, touching his hand.

He nodded, then grabbed my hand and drew me to him and held me close. The smell of dust and an unpleasant fustiness permeated his overalls. I turned my head so I didn't have to breathe it in. This wasn't Will. He was calm in almost any crisis. Whatever was down there must be bad.

Finally he let me go. "I need a drink."

"Scotch?" I asked, already halfway out of the room.

He nodded. "Neat, No ice or water. Bring the bottle." He glanced back at the hole in the wall "No, wait. I'm coming with you."

In the living room, our overalls and masks discarded in the hall, I poured drinks for both of us. We sat and I noticed Will perched on the edge of his seat. He was jumpy. On edge.

He took a large swig, grabbed the bottle and topped himself up. In the space of a few minutes he had consumed more Scotch than he would normally get through in a month. Another hefty swig and he was ready.

"Okay. It's a dark, almost empty room. There's a wooden table. Plain, nothing fancy, covered in dust and stuff. Then, in the center of the space, on the floor there's a large iron ring. Attached to that are four sets of manacles, enough to tether four people—by the feet, I'm guessing. There's a lot of wax and burned-out candles around—big ones. Lots on the table. They're like the sort you get in church at Easter. Then, on the far wall, which I think runs under the library, there's a kind of altar, covered in a dark cloth. It looks the worse for wear. Probably not been touched for years. Above it, there's a complete goat's skull. Horns and all. The altar cloth.... I moved it a little. It's floor length. Underneath..." He took yet another swig and said nothing.

"Tell me, Will. Please. Whatever it is."

He looked up at me and I had never seen such horror reflected in anyone's eyes, let alone Will's. "Di. We have to call the police. There's a body under there."

Chapter Ten

The police let us go down there the next day, after the body had been removed but while their lighting was still rigged up. Will was reluctant but I insisted. If he didn't see the place in proper light—and without the corpse—his lingering memory of it would be the last thing he saw. The police officer was a friendly, chatty soul. A detective inspector, he'd worked on serious crime for ten years. We wouldn't believe the stuff he'd seen, he said. Reassuringly he informed us that the forensic pathologist was certain this person had died at least a century before. Not so reassuringly, he told us she was pretty sure that death was not from natural causes.

"Judging by the paraphernalia down there it was probably of a ritual nature. There's all sorts of stories of weird stuff going on here and up at the abbey. Looks like some of it may even be true."

"Is there any way of knowing who the victim was? Was it a male or female?" I asked.

"Female definitely. Young woman, probably in her early twenties. Can't tell an awful lot more until the pathologist gets her on the table and examines the bones. No trace of any clothing so we can assume she was placed down there naked. Or maybe she crawled in, trying to escape. Difficult to tell. But there's no need to worry. Whoever did that to her is long gone. Dead, buried and forgotten about. And now, thanks to you, she'll get a decent burial. No name, but she can rest in peace at long last. That should lay any restless ghost to rest, shouldn't it?" He laughed and went on his way. I wished I could join him, both in his mirth and his getaway.

Three days later, work recommenced on the library but, at the request of the police, we didn't do anything about boarding up the doorway until they had completed their investigations. The pathologist had been able to determine that it was highly likely the young woman's throat had been cut. The bones had been almost completely severed in her neck by a sharp blade. We were no closer to knowing when she had been murdered or if she had died in situ although it seemed likely.

"The fact that someone thought to make a doorway, with a keyhole, suggests they still wanted access to the downstairs room," our friendly policeman said. "So they may have kept people down there themselves, or been responsible for this young woman's death, or wanted to venerate her as some sort of relic from the past. We may never know. Fascinating though, isn't it?"

If it hadn't been here, I might have also thought it merely fascinating but, for the time being, this was the place I laid my head every night. Once again, the idea of moving to a hotel appealed. His suggestion of this young victim being some sort of religious relic didn't sit well either, but for different reasons. If he was right, why wasn't she enshrined in some way?

When I hung up, I shared what he'd said with Will. Since his gory discovery he had been noticeably subdued. He didn't seem to want to stay in the house much and kept going off on his own for walks. When I suggested I accompany him he declined. "It's nothing, Di. I'm sorry, I just want to be alone for an hour, that's all."

He didn't volunteer any information on where he walked to and only gave vague answers when I asked him. "Just over the moors for a while. Nowhere in particular."

I was busy with the house so didn't pursue it, but I did resent it. This place was entirely his idea. *His* project except for my post-purchase involvement in décor. Yet it was me that had to do all the liaising with Mick and the decorators, electricians, plumbers and every other brand of tradesperson on the planet. When I asked for Will's opinion, he had nothing to say anymore. I wanted to challenge him but bit my tongue. He seemed to be fighting his own demons and if I pestered him, he would only push me away. I suppose I should have been grateful that this at least showed he probably wasn't going to kick up much of a fuss about selling up and moving. I consoled myself with this but, right at that moment with all the work going on before we could reasonably expect to have any chance of getting a decent price for the place, it didn't help much. He was shutting me out for the first time in our life together and I hated it. Worst of all, I felt lonely. And vulnerable.

In the library, Mick propped the old door against the hole. Its smell might have dissipated but the sight of its ominous black presence sent shivers up my spine. At least this way we didn't have to look at it.

I managed to get Trevor on his own one sunny morning when I asked to borrow him to help with a blocked sink. I knew what he would find because I had purposely stuffed it with a mixture of congealed fat from the roast lamb at the weekend, tea leaves and various other detritus. I handed him the plunger and Marigolds and he got to work. After an icebreaker of niceties about the weather had resulted in some semblance of conversation between us, I took my own plunge.

"What did you make of what we found under the library?" I asked.

He paused in his efforts and stared straight ahead through the window for a few seconds. "Me Mam said they did things like that," he said, at last.

"You mean sacrifices?"

He nodded.

"What about what you saw? The ghost? I believe you, by the way. I've had my own experiences here."

He turned his gaze to me, his eyes seeming to search mine for any trace I was mocking him. Apparently reassured he continued, "She were a nun. She were scared of summat and she went right through me. It were dead cold that. When she went through me."

"I'm sure it was. Did you feel anything else when she went through you? Did you pick up anything from her?"

"She were pregnant," he said, resuming his plunging. "And she were that scared they were going to kill her and t'baby when it came out of her. That's all. Then she were gone, but me Mam said we were related to the man that built this house. Not the first one. The second. A right nasty piece of work, Mam calls him."

"Do you know his name?"

"Aye. It were Samuel Clitheroe. And he were t'direct descendant of that Matilda so we're related to her too. A right rum lot we are." He laughed nervously then glanced over his shoulder. Then he summoned me closer. "I don't want to speak too loud, but this house isn't right. Mam doesn't like me coming here. If Uncle Mick didn't pay me she wouldn't let me come. I don't know how you can live here with all that going on. The ghosts and the...you know, what your husband found down them stairs."

I matched his whispers. "Don't you worry, Trevor. I've already told Will. As soon as this place is finished we're out of here. This house is going up for sale. Frankly I'm not even bothered if we make any money on it. I just want it gone." His expression screamed confusion. "What is it, Trevor?"

"I've probably got it wrong. Mam always says I get the wrong end of t'stick. But I heard Mr. Clarke tell Uncle Mick yesterday that he loves it 'ere and he never wants to leave. He said he'd persuade you to love it too."

"What?" Surely he had got it wrong.

"Well, that's what Uncle Mick said anyway. He said he thought it was plain daft. " 'They could live almost anywhere they like,' he said to me Mam. 'And they choose that godforsaken hole.' Honest, Mrs. Clarke, I'm not making it up. That's what he said."

"I don't doubt that's what you heard, Trevor. I'll speak to my husband. Set him straight about a few things."

Trevor finished unblocking the sink, mostly in silence, and returned to help Mick in the library. Will returned soon after and I collared him in the kitchen. I shut the doors, not wanting to create a spectacle although my temper was at boiling point.

Will offloaded fresh meat and vegetables. I launched into him. "Why did you tell Mick we were going to stay here after the place is finished?"

"You have to admit it's coming on a treat now the restoration work's done. You've chosen some lovely colors. Who wouldn't fall in love with this place?"

"Me for starters. Will, however much we tart this place up, it is with one end in sight. Selling it for the best price we can get which, considering its reputation and isolated location may not be nearly as easy as it was for the previous vendor. I'm counting the days 'til we can hand the keys over. What part of that don't you understand?"

The incredulous look on his face told me the answer before he opened his mouth. "I can't believe you're saying that, Di. You've put so much into this."

"Only to get it finished as quickly as possible. It gives me the creeps. Every room in this house turns my stomach. And the skeleton under the library was the final straw. Mick can't understand why on earth we would want to stay here. Trevor's bloody terrified of some ghostly nun who keeps haunting him.... Oh, and did you know he's related to the builder of this place? Some guy called Samuel Clitheroe apparently."

"No, I didn't know that but Corinne mentioned Samuel Clitheroe."

"And what did she say about him?"

Will shrugged. "Nothing. Just said he was the builder."

"He was a lot more than that. Trevor told me he was a villain. I don't know the details, but I'm going to find out. I can bet he knew exactly what he was doing when he bought this land. Why else would he preserve that room—and put a door in the false wall with a key? He was the one who used it. The bookcases were installed much later by someone who didn't want that place ever found or used again. My guess is Clitheroe was a devil worshiper and probably knew something about the woman under the altar. Maybe he even put her there himself."

"For heaven's sake, Di. You're talking about some nutter from over two hundred years ago. More probably. All that lot are long dead and buried. Whatever they did died along with them. That poor woman.... We have no idea who she was. She may even have been deluded enough to give herself willingly as a sacrifice."

"What? Who willingly submits to having their throat cut?"

"It has been known. I'm sure I read about it somewhere—"

"Don't be so fucking stupid, Will. And, frankly, even if you're right, it makes no difference to how I feel. This place is ugly in a way no amount of fancy furnishings will ever conceal. Its stones are soaked in some vile memories of despicable practices that took place here—"

"Get a priest in."

"What?"

"Get a priest in. Get someone in to perform an exorcism. Wave a load of smoking sage brushes around and cleanse the house of evil spirits if it makes you feel better."

"Don't be ridiculous."

"I'm not. You're the one talking about ghosts and the building being infested with some sort of images from the past. That's the way to deal with them. Priests, exorcisms, prayers, holy water. Phone the local Catholic church and ask them."

He turned back to his shopping, busying himself with putting celery, carrots and potatoes in the salad drawer of the fridge while I stared at his back.

"Will, this isn't going away. I'm not living here."

He spun on his heel. "Then we have a problem. Because I am."

Chapter Eleven

Living in a world of stony silences has never been my way. I prefer to have one blazing row, get everything out in the open and then move on—perhaps with the added benefit of a passionate making up. I always thought it was mine and Will's way too. But not this time. This time he was closed. It was like living with a virtual stranger. If I entered a room, he left it. Meals were especially fraught. We sat at opposite ends of a long, mahogany dining table that I discovered under a tarpaulin and barely a word was exchanged beyond a request to pass the salt.

When I sat down and went through all the paperwork Will had been given when the sale completed, I found evidence that the house had changed hands many times, in rapid succession after Samuel Clitheroe's time. There were many gaps, indicating either periods when the house was unoccupied or people who had come and gone without leaving a single trace they had ever lived here. Lots of paperwork, but nothing that made me any the wiser as to their reasons for their short occupation.

The only people I spoke to during the next three days were Mick and Trevor and as the fourth day began much as the previous three had ended, I rounded on Will when he opened the kitchen door on his way out.

"Will, we can't go on like this," I said.

He hesitated, seemingly unsure whether to ignore me and keep going or stop and face it out. He chose the latter, but didn't let go of the door.

"There's not a lot to discuss, is there?" he said and the hostility was clear. "You've made your mind up you're not staying and I've decided I am. Seems like we're at an impasse. Either one of us gives way or..." He let the sentence hang.

"Or what?" I demanded. "Are you saying we're done here? Just like that? Over this fucking house? What does that say about us, Will?"

"I really don't know Diana. What do you think it says about us? *I* bought a house with huge potential that *you're* starting to fulfill. Look at this place compared with the ruin it was before. Your designs and ideas, the workmanship of the guys we've hired. How can you walk away from all that to live in some tatty little two-bedroom cottage?"

"That wasn't my choice either, if you remember. You decided that too, *you* decided to sell our home without telling me. In fact, you're the one making all the decisions this past few months. Well now I've made one and I'm not budging from it. You knew how I felt all along and you agreed to it. You're the one reneging on a deal. Not me. I've told you what I've experienced and I'm not the only one. Have you spoken to Trevor?"

Will laughed. "That lad wouldn't know a ghost from a real person. Mick told me. He's got mental problems. Lack of oxygen at birth or something. Nice enough boy but you can't rely on what he says. He imagines things. Always has. Mick said when Trevor was a child he had an imaginary friend only, in his case, the friend lasted well into his teens."

"And what's your excuse for me then? He and I have pretty much seen the same thing only Trevor's experience was more intense than mine. Maybe his condition makes him more open and receptive to psychic phenomena."

"Look, Di, I've no idea what you think you saw. It's an old house with a lot of atmosphere and a shedload of legends. It's bound to play on anyone's mind."

"Except yours apparently."

"And Mick's, and probably a host of others. That's irrelevant. You'd be best not to keep asking Trevor questions. The answers are likely to mix you up even more."

"Oh, great! Now I'm the little wife who needs protecting from her hysterical woman's mind."

"Come on, Di. You know perfectly well that's not what I meant."

"Didn't you? Really? I'm not so sure, Will, because right now I'm not sure who you are anymore. You're not the Will I know. The Will I know would have given some credence to what I said and wouldn't have been so fucking pigheaded."

"Yeah? And the Diana I know wouldn't keep losing her temper and behaving like a fucking harridan."

"*Harridan?*" My voice had risen a few decibels and I became aware we were not alone. Trevor was watching, white-faced and scared, from the doorway into the hall. "Yes, what is it, Trevor?" I asked, after lowering my voice and plastering on a reassuring smile.

Trevor blinked and visibly swallowed. "Uncle Mick says…" he coughed. "Uncle Mick says, is it all right with you if we knock off at lunchtime, only he needs to take me Mam to the hospital for her physiotherapy?"

"Yes, of course, Trevor. I didn't know she was having treatment."

"It's her hip. It got displaced when she was having me and it's never been right since. She walks with a limp nowadays and they're trying to help her."

"Hope it works," Will said.

"Thank you, Mr. Clarke. Mrs. Clarke." He backed off.

Will didn't hang around. I was still staring after Trevor when the door slammed and he was gone. The car engine started a few moments later.

After lunch, I found myself entirely alone in the house, a rare if not unique occurrence. There had usually been someone there, whether it be Mick, Trevor, Derek or one of the other workmen, or Will. Who knew when he would be back?

The sun was shining on a beautiful day. I could have gone outside and pottered about in what had once been a small front garden. Or I could stay inside and attempt to confront my fears.

I chose the latter.

If I were to convince Will we should sell up and leave as soon as the work was completed, I needed evidence. The police had finished with the room below the library but I hadn't. Maybe down there was something that would help me understand the nature of this place. Perhaps there was something tangible I could show Will that would support my claims about the house he was so determined to make his home.

I took out the flashlight from under the sink and tested it. The beam was strong and full. I grabbed my phone. Photographic evidence would be irrefutable. I had only charged it the previous night as I usually did. I was ready.

In the library, the old door was still propped against the wall. Fortunately it wasn't too heavy and I was able to shove it along far enough for me to squeeze in. I switched on the flashlight and crossed over. The smell of fustiness and damp earth tickled my nostrils but at least the awful smell of decay and decomposition were no longer there. I took the few steps to the tops of the steps and shone the beam downwards, then, with a first tentative step I began my descent.

Being stone, the steps were firm and were barely worn as if not too many people had used them. Whatever this place had been it had clearly been intended only for an elite, or hadn't been used over a long period.

I kept my left hand on the wall, to steady me. The stone felt cold and dry at first, tending towards a slight clamminess the further I descended. I counted the steps in my head. After ten, I could see the bottom clearly. Eighteen and I was there. I flashed the beam all around. The shackles attached to the large iron ring in the center of the stone floor reflected in the light. The silence of the underground room, along with its coldness, made me shiver.

I shone the flashlight at the far side of the wall where I knew the altar to be. The suddenness of the goat skull made me cry out. I reminded myself I knew it would be there but the reality of being confronted with it still chilled me to the core. My phone was in my pocket. I removed it, opened up the camera and fired off half a dozen or more rapid shots all around me. Maybe I wouldn't get another chance. It wouldn't take much to spook me down there. Hell, I was already spooked and nothing had happened.

I pocketed my phone and made my way across the uneven floor, taking care not to trip over the chains. In the full glare of the flashlight, I could make out that the altar cloth was velvet and had once been purple, now covered in layers of dust, dirt and general debris, disturbed by the recent forensic work. Taking courage in both hands, I pulled the cloth aside to reveal underneath. Dark staining and a residual stench of decay made my stomach clench and I dropped the cloth back in place.

A small but sudden noise broke the silence and I caught my breath, A mouse? I listened hard. Nothing. And then...a slight, low moan. That was no mouse.

A breath on my ear. Something close by. I daren't move. Whispers. Someone speaking, reciting maybe. A prayer? Not in English. It sounded like Latin. I couldn't make anything out.

Please, God, let me get out of here in one piece.

The voice stopped. Something like an invisible hand brushed my arm and dropped away. But still I felt a presence close by. Then the sensation drained away. I dared to look over my shoulder and flashed the beam into the blackness. Nothing there. But my courage had deserted me. Whatever Will said, I had felt that—whatever it was. It was real. I hadn't imagined it.

I raced up the stairs and back into the relative normality of the library. I pushed the door back into place and staggered backward into the room.

Just in time to see the tall figure of a nun disappear out of the corner of my eye.

Chapter Twelve

"I tell you that's what happened, Will. I know what I felt and I know what I saw." We were in the living room, shortly after he arrived back, facing each other like two combatants.

"You were scared. It's horrible, I know. I was there, remember? I was the one who found that body. It's bound to play on your mind. I don't know why the hell you went down there in the first place."

"To try and get something to show you I'm not imagining things."

"And what did you actually find?"

What had I found? Nothing. Not one shred of evidence that the place was haunted or cursed or anything that would show it posed some sort of danger to anyone.

"I took some photographs. I haven't checked them yet."

"Okay, well let's have a look then."

I opened the camera app on my phone and selected the first. It was blurry, with a gray shadow obliterating anything identifiable. I skipped to the next and the one after that and so on until I had finished. All were the same.

"This can't be right," I said. "It's like someone threw some sort of cloak over the camera."

"Let me see."

I handed Will the phone. I saw him swipe from one to the other. He handed me back the phone. "Looks like you had your hand over the lens the whole time."

"But I didn't," I said and went through them again. "Maybe something else did."

Will gave a derisory snort. "I'm sorry, Di, but you're going to have to do better than that." His tone was so unlike him. Will was never hostile like this. Why now? What had happened to him since we had been here that he could change like this? What—or who?

"Where did you go today?" I asked.

"Went out for a drive and then a walk over the moors."

"Where?"

"I don't know. Just pulled into a layby and set off. It's a beautiful day."

I glanced down at his feet. He was barefoot. "Which shoes did you wear?"

"My trainers. Look, what is this? An inquisition?"

"No. I just wondered if you met anyone. Out walking I mean. You were gone a long time. Nearly three hours."

"It didn't seem like it. And no, I didn't meet anyone."

"Did you go anywhere near the old abbey?"

"Not far. I could see it. Look, Diana, if you're trying to accuse me of something, come right out with it. I don't like these games of twenty questions."

"It's no game, Will. I'm serious. You've changed. Since we got here, you're not the same and I hate every bit of it. This new Will isn't the man I married. You can't deny it. You're different and I think you're under some influence or other. Who's causing it I have no idea but—"

Will grabbed the nearest thing—a small crystal vase on the mantlepiece—and flung it. It smashed against the wall. "Enough! Stop this right now, Diana. I've had enough of this constant haranguing. Unfounded accusations, crazy talk about ghosts and hauntings. You need help, and I mean it. You need medical help. There's something wrong with you. Do you want a divorce? Is that it? Do you want us to break up and this is your way of doing it? Well, go on, answer me?"

I tried. I opened my mouth and tried to speak but the words wouldn't come out. Because right at that moment, over his left shoulder a figure I knew couldn't be real was grinning at me.

Chapter Thirteen

I pointed, my finger shaking uncontrollably. Will looked at me as if I had sprouted another head.

"What's the matter now? What's wrong with you? What are you pointing at?" He glanced over his shoulder but, of course, the…whatever it was…vanished.

I let my hand fall.

"Well, are you going to answer me or what?"

"I know you're not going to believe me but just now there was some kind of… I don't know…*creature*. I don't know what it was. It looked like…. Like one of those illustrations in Grimm's Fairy Tales. It was sort of floating above your shoulder…a grinning head, massive eyes, misshapen ears, long, skinny arms like twigs. And then it was gone. It didn't want you to see it so it went when you turned to look at it."

Will stared at me. "Do you know how crazy you sound right now?"

I nodded. "I know it sounds mad, but that's what I saw."

"You need serious help." He took his phone out of his pocket.

"What are you doing?"

"I'm going to call the NHS helpline."

"No, Will, don't. That's not the answer. I'm not the only one seeing things here. Look, get your priest. See if an exorcism works. Maybe it will. Maybe we can get the demons out of this place once and for all."

Will hesitated. For a second, I caught a look of something approaching compassion in his eyes and it made me realize how long that, or anything remotely like it, had been missing from my husband.

He glanced down at his phone and began scrolling.

"What are you doing?"

He didn't look up from the screen. "Calling Corinne. She might know a local priest who can perform the ceremony or whatever they call it."

Involving Corinne wasn't my first choice but at least Will wasn't having me sectioned…yet.

She answered almost immediately and a rapid exchange followed. When he ended the call, he tucked his phone back in his jeans pocket and treated me to a rare smile.

"It's good news and bad news. The bad news is that Corinne said it can take weeks or longer to get a proper priest out. The good news is that she knows someone. She's a sort of white witch. Handy with a sage brush, the right chants and so forth. She can cleanse your house and banish the evil spirits. Corinne's going to call her—" His phone rang. "That's her now."

Another quick call. An arrangement to meet the next day. End of call.

"Her name's Leah and she's coming over tomorrow at around eleven. I'll phone Mick and tell him not to start back here until after two. All being well, by tomorrow afternoon, you won't see any more goblins, gremlins or evil nuns."

I bit my tongue. There was so much I could have said but it would have made no difference. Will was convinced I was delusional and this was his one attempt to get me to drop my resistance to this house. For the sake of both my sanity and my marriage I prayed it worked.

I woke suddenly as if something had disturbed me. It was pitch dark and silent. The windows were closed so I couldn't even hear any of the usual night sounds like the distant hoot of an owl or the lonely bark of a fox. I turned over and plumped up the pillow but sleep eluded me. Beside me, Will slept on, his deep rhythmic breathing steady. The more I lay there trying to sleep the more my brain refused to shut down. If I sat up and tried to read, I would wake Will. He was grumpy when his sleep was disturbed at the best of times and these were far from the best of times. There was only one thing for it. I pushed back the covers and slid out of bed.

Once outside the bedroom, I made sure I switched on all the lights as I made my way along the hallway to the landing. Downstairs loomed dark and uninviting until I pressed the light switch and the hall lights came on. Now I could see there was nothing lurking in the shadows and, my feet encased in warm slippers, I tied my robe closer around me and made my way down. Keeping the lights on, I went into the kitchen with the intention of making a cup of tea, but that's when I heard the sobbing.

It was soft at first, like a small animal snuffling. I followed the sound and it led me into the library. Moonlight poured in through the windows, slashing a swathe of pale luminescence across the floor where, at the far end, bathed in a strange, ethereal glow, a young woman gazed over at me, her face contorted by sadness. I felt drawn to her in a way I couldn't control. It was as if my feet controlled me. Within seconds, I was directly in front of her. Her eyes were dark and grew darker still as she stared at me, then through me. Without warning, she screamed—her mouth an open, black hole into which I sank, my spirit caught up in the unearthly, terrible cry that seemed wrenched from a thousand souls in torment. It wrapped me, smothered me. I tried to cover my ears against it but I had no body to obey me. All I had was my spirit, my soul, and that was disappearing fast down this bottomless pit of despair. The sensation of falling was physical, like being on a rapidly depressurizing, plunging aircraft.

And then it was over.

I came to on a cold, stone floor, in almost total darkness save for the flickering light of a couple of tall candles a few feet away. In a second I realized I wasn't alone.

All around me, figures emerged from nowhere, dressed alike in nuns' habits. But one stood apart. A tall male. He was garbed in black and stood between the two candles which I now saw were mounted in an elaborate candelabra and standing on an altar. Somehow, the room grew a little lighter so I could make out that I was the only one who took no physical form. I was no longer on the floor but floating, at the same level as the heads of the group that appeared to be some sort of congregation involved in a Mass. No one seemed to realize I was there. Except the man in the black robes.

His face was one I would never forget. Pale skin, dark beard, eyes black as night. He removed a key from his sleeve and opened a box I recognized; it was identical to the one Will had found discarded in one of the outbuildings and, with everything else going on, I had forgotten about. He took something from it and raised it. A golden goblet that glinted in the candlelight. At the sight of it, the assembled sighed and fell to their knees before prostrating themselves before him. He spoke in a language that sounded similar to what I had heard in the library when the whispering had come to me. I couldn't make any of it out but it sounded disjointed as if someone was playing a recording backwards. The odd word sounded vaguely Latin but I could make out nothing more than that.

The man lowered the goblet and the people stood, silent, waiting. Then one moved forward. She approached him and I watched as he took her robe in his hands and wrenched it off her, letting it slide to the ground. She made no protest. He then turned her around to face the people. An appreciative sigh went up from them at the sight of this young and beautiful naked woman, her long dark hair hanging over her shoulders and below her full breasts.

A wave of horror shot through me as I realized what I was witnessing but was powerless to prevent. And this man knew that. He wanted me to watch. He had arranged it that way. The girl couldn't have been more than sixteen years old yet she was calm and appeared willing. She smiled as the man fondled her breasts from behind. I was aware of movement from some of the assembled and, from the motions, I guessed they were males and they were masturbating. Hoods obscured both their faces and their gender but the hand motions through their thin robes were unmistakable. Moans of ecstasy from some echoed around the room. The man turned the girl around to face him and lifted her onto the altar. Meeting no resistance from her, he spread her legs and lifted his robe. In a swift motion, he thrust himself at her and she gave a cry of pain as he entered her. Again and again, to the cries of appreciation from his disciples, he thrust harder and harder. The girl's cries only seemed to spur him and the crowd on. Then, with a mighty roar, he climaxed and pulled out of her, stepping aside so the people could see the carnage of blood and more that poured from the girl who lay, apparently unconscious, on the altar.

The assembled cheered, threw off their robes and revealed their nakedness. Not all were as beautiful as the defiled and bleeding girl who stirred and moaned, but all were blind in their lust, wanting one thing and finding it in a willing partner. Lacking a body, I couldn't even look away. The demonic parody of a priest stared hard at me, a hideous grin on his face that I had seen before on the face of that creature looking over Will's shoulder. He had covered himself now but not before I glimpsed the still partially erect, massive penis, covered in small barbs. He must have torn the girl to shreds. It certainly explained the quantity of blood that still flowed in a steady stream from her vagina.

All around the room, couples were climaxing and the noises of the orgy abated as they rearranged their robes around themselves.

Their host raised a sword that gleamed in the candlelight. It was curved, its handle golden. As the man brought it down, it flashed once. The girl gave one partial scream and went silent. There was a pause. He raised the dripping weapon and the throng cheered. He drank in the adulation of his followers, then cast me a contemptuous stare, pointed the sword at me and everything darkened.

Chapter Fourteen

I woke with a start in my bed. It was morning, the drapes were open and Will was nowhere to be seen. I sat up and rubbed my eyes. Was that really only a nightmare?

I pushed back the covers and stepped into my slippers. The memory of what I had witnessed—or dreamt—stayed with me as I showered and dressed. Downstairs I heard Will talking to someone and only then did I realize what the time was. Eleven-thirty. Leah.

The pervading aroma of burning herbs—sage predominantly—led me to the living room where a tall woman with bright red hair, dressed in jeans and a T-shirt bearing the Wiccan symbol of a pentagram, was wafting a sage brush around and chanting. At various junctures around the room, small bowls gently smoldered, their aromatic contents not unpleasant and vaguely reminiscent of the smell I remembered from old, small Catholic churches. I stood quietly on the threshold until she had finished. Her eyes were closed in a final prayer, uttered in yet another language I didn't understand but which bore some vague resemblance to English.

When she finished, she opened her eyes and gave me a long, hard stare.

"Hello," I said, as brightly as I could manage. "I'm Diana. You must be Leah."

She didn't smile. "Yes, you are, and yes I am." Now she smiled. "I'm cleansing your house."

"I just hope it works. It's been hell."

"Of course it has. You have evil here. But I have never failed yet so don't worry. Houses are not so hard. People though. Ah, yes, people can be tricky." Her voice was tinged with a slight accent. Eastern European of some kind.

She seemed to read my mind. "I am from Romania. We know what it is like to share your home with unwanted spirits. When we move house we always ask the priest to cleanse our home. I was surprised when I come here, to England, you don't do it. It is no surprise you have so much trouble with the undead."

It was reassuring to be taken seriously but the way she kept staring at me was less so. Will was watching, seemingly enjoying the interaction.

"What language was that?" I asked. "Romanian?"

"No. It was English but old. Your writer, Chaucer, would have spoken it. I find it works best with demons in this country. I don't know why but it is an old trick someone taught me."

"I'm amazed you can speak it. I always had trouble with the language when we did *The Canterbury Tales* at school."

"Oh, I can't. I only know the prayers. But you, you have heard another language recently, haven't you?"

"How do you know that?"

"Because I see it in your eyes. You have encountered the evil in this house and it spoke to you. It used the Latin but not the right way."

"Backwards?" Because it suddenly became clear.

"Yes. A devil's trick. Not very subtle."

"How do you know this? About me, I mean?" I glanced at Will but his stony gaze gave nothing away. He was standing on the far side of the room, arms folded. He looked like a stranger. I turned back to Leah.

"My mother said it was a gift," she said, "Sometimes it feels like a curse, but I can tell what goes on here." She tapped her forehead. "In your case, it screams at me and fills my head."

"I'm not going crazy then?"

Leah shook her head. "If you are, then so am I. And I know that I am not."

The relief was like a tidal wave. I could have kissed her. "Thank you, Leah. I really needed to hear that. I need to speak with you. Things are happening. Last night—" I suddenly realized Will wasn't there. I had moved further into the room and he must have slipped out behind me when I was concentrating on Leah. "Excuse me one second," I said. "Please carry on. I need to find Will."

Leah nodded and, as I raced out of the library, I was just in time to see Will driving off down the drive. He failed to stop when I shot out of the door, waving my arms frantically.

How do you go from elation to despair in one second flat? I can tell you it's possible because it happened to me. Right then. Frustration. Anger. Sorrow. Tears streamed down my cheeks. I grabbed at a large stone and hurled it. I didn't hear it land. I told myself to pull myself together; to get back inside and talk to Leah.

I took deep cleansing breaths of fresh moorland air and listened for a few moments to the wind whistling through the long grass. In no more than a few seconds, it blew distant aromas of sheep droppings from the farm, a bee buzzed close to my face, two large white butterflies danced, birds sang and the sun emerged from behind a white fluffy cloud. I stared across at the distant peaks of the Pennines. All of this happened as nature dictated. It had all existed long before me and would continue long after me. It encompassed the past, present and future. Constant. All else would pass. All else...transient.

My thoughts renewed my courage and restored a little perspective to my increasingly insane, unreal world. I made my way back into the house and caught up with Leah upstairs on the landing.

"I am finished up here," she said. "This house is...challenging. I may have to return. I think you will find things have improved but perhaps not everywhere. There is something I am missing and I am not sure.... Are there any rooms I have not seen yet?"

"Did Will tell you about the room below the library? Its entrance is behind the old door propped up at the far end of the room."

She shook her head, "I asked him about that and he said it was not necessary. That it was not a room."

"What? Of course it's a room. I've been down there and so has he. It's probably the source of all the trouble here. Come with me, Leah, please. I think it may answer your concerns. Or add to them. We'll need some light though. I'll only be a minute." I dashed into the kitchen and retrieved the flashlight. I raced back to join Leah.

She said nothing, picked up two of her still-smoking bowls and handed me one. In her other hand, the cleansing sage brush smoldered.

"You'll need one hand free to steady yourself down the steps," I said. "To be on the safe side."

She balanced the bowl and sage brush in one hand and followed me. Once over the threshold, the now familiar fusty dampness filled my nostrils.

Leah gasped. "What is this place?"

"You'll see." I switched on the beam and guided us down the steps. At each descent. I heard Leah catch her breath. At the bottom, I shone the light on her. Her eyes were wide, like a frightened and cornered animal.

She moistened her lips. "There is great evil here. This is the beating black heart of this house." She looked at her sage brush and the bowl. "I feel I am about to confront Goliath and I only have two small stones and no sling."

The chilling dampness enveloped me like a cloak and I shivered. "Is there nothing you can do here? I mean, in the story, David had pretty much what you said and he beat Goliath."

Leah gave a half-smile and shrugged. "All I can do, I will, but I fear it is not enough." She laid down the bowl on the altar and I was certain I heard a hiss. From her reaction—a slight jump back—I knew Leah had registered something too. The air was heavier as if waiting for something, or someone. to emerge.

With a shaking arm, Leah raised her hand and wafted the sage brush, chanting all the while. I kept the flashlight as still as I was able yet the shadows danced on the wall in its reflection, their shapes taking on the form of dancing nuns and I was transported back to my nightmare. But how could I continue to believe that a part of me hadn't been transported here last night? For a second, I was back there; my spirit devoid of body as it had been. I had heard of astral projection but always dismissed it. Now though…

Another hiss from the altar. Louder this time. I shone the flashlight on it.

"The bowl," I cried. "It's not smoking."

Leah stopped in mid-chant and checked it. She touched the bowl. "Stone cold." Mine had been quite hot. I had needed to keep my hand off the bottom when I transported it down the steps. I picked it up. It was so cold, my hand almost stuck to it

"We are not here alone," Leah said. "We must go. Now." She fled back to the steps and began to mount them. I dashed after her but stopped short of the bottom of the stairwell. Something was pushing against me. I shone the flashlight wildly around. When the beam illuminated the steps I saw Leah slumped unconscious. I struggled to get to her but the force was too strong. Then light appeared at the top of the stairs. Two people, each holding flashlights. A familiar male voice. I couldn't place him at first.

"Diana. What's going on here?"

Then I remembered. That public school clipped tone. Laurence.

"Thank God you're there," I called. "Leah's fainted. Please help us." With a mighty effort, I lurched forward. Whatever had held me there had let go.

Laurence handed his flashlight to his companion. She was still in shadow but I guessed who it was.

"How odd," Corinne said. "I never knew this was here until Will told me you'd found it. Now I see it for myself it's even stranger than I imagined."

I had no time for her ruminations. "We've got to help Leah," I said, as I patted her cheeks and tried to find a pulse on her ice-cold wrist. She stirred, opened her eyes and instantly struggled to sit up.

"It's all right, Leah," Laurence said. "You took a tumble but you're okay now. Let's get you back upstairs."

Leah allowed him to lift her and we guided her up the stairs, Laurence leading and me bringing up the rear.

Corinne waited at the top, shining the flashlights to illuminate our way.

"I'll call an ambulance," I said.

Corinne made a harrumphing noise. "No point. Unless Leah's had a heart attack or a stroke or something they won't be here for hours. If she needs hospital treatment it's far better one of us takes her to Leeds in the car."

"I don't need a hospital," Leah said, her voice exhausted. "A glass of water would be good though."

"Brandy?" I suggested.

Leah shook her head. "No. I do not touch alcohol. It is bad for my head."

By the time I returned with a full glass of Evian, Leah was lying on the settee in the living room where Laurence had carried her. Apart from a few dirty marks on her jeans and looking as if a few hours' sleep wouldn't come amiss, she appeared unhurt.

Laurence and Corinne were sitting on nearby easy chairs. I handed Leah the water and knelt beside her. Her hands shook as she accepted the glass from me so I steadied her while she sipped.

"What were you two doing down there?" Corinne asked.

"It was part of Leah's cleansing ritual." I said. "It was the last place left."

"Pretty gruesome," Laurence said. "That room. From what I saw of it anyway."

"It is much more than that." Leah said, refusing any more water. "There is a beast down there."

I stared at her. "A beast?"

"I must explain. A beast is what I call a devil of great power. The one down there—in this house—is the worst I have ever encountered. Once it lived as a human but its humanity left it long before mortal life did. I know the rumors about this place and I am sorry to say you have opened up the worst of them. It has been bad enough before. Now it is..." She shook her head.

"Come on, Leah," Corinne said. "I mean this house cleansing stuff. I go along with it because the punters like it and it makes me some money. I thought you felt the same."

"When have I ever said that?" Leah swung her legs off the settee. "You should know better, Corinne. You of all people."

"Why her 'of all people,' Leah?" I asked and then turned to Corinne and Laurence. "And what were the two of you doing here in the first place?"

"I'll go first, shall I?" Corinne said. "I have no idea what Leah means and I'll leave it to her to explain herself. As for us, we have a meeting with your husband in…" She checked her watch. "Any minute now. He's late. We rang the bell, there was no reply so we let ourselves in and heard a noise from the library."

Leah sat up fully. "And I mean that Corinne is a direct descendant of Samuel Clitheroe who built this house on the ruins of the one erected by Matilda de Talamund. He was a disciple of Afagddu ap Llewellyn. A few of them lingered on, meeting in secret to conduct their foul rituals including human sacrifice, right up until at least sometime in the nineteenth century or even later."

"Is that true, Corinne? You really are related to that vile bastard?"

Corinne's expression was granite-like. "We all have our skeletons in the closet. If you dig around long and far enough, every family has a Samuel Clitheroe somewhere in their dim and distant past."

"I doubt that," Leah said. "He was the devil incarnate and he is still here. His spirit infests this house along with Brother Alfred and Matilda."

"I heard this Llewellyn creature forced Matilda to sacrifice their baby," I said.

Leah's laugh was mirthless. "Forced? Let me ask you this then. Did Alan Brady force Myra Hindley to torture, murder and bury those children on the moors back in the Sixties?"

"No," I agreed. "Some say she was the main instigator."

"Or at the very least his enabler," Leah said. "Matilda was as guilty as her lover and generations later, Samuel was a willing apprentice."

The sound of a car engine. Will was back at last. I jumped up and went to greet him. We met in the hall. He seemed distracted, looking all around, before grabbing my shoulders. He squeezed so hard I winced but he didn't lessen his grip.

"Where's Corinne?" It was a demand, not a question.

"She's in the living room with—" But he had already gone. I followed.

In front of my disbelieving eyes, he strode over to Corinne. She stood, a triumphant smile on her face. I couldn't understand why. Ten seconds later, I knew.

She opened her arms to him. My husband. As if in a nightmare, I watched the person who had been the center of my world gather this woman in his arms and kiss her passionately. I stared. Laurence stared. Only Leah seemed unfazed. She stood, a little uncertainly, swayed a fraction and held onto the arm of the settee for balance.

Corinne and Will came out of their clinch and the action forced me out of my shocked trance.

"What the hell is going on?" I heard myself ask.

"Isn't it obvious?" Corinne asked, running her hand down Will's arm. "We're in love."

Will kissed the tip of her nose. "I'm sorry you found out this way, Di, but it had to come out one day. Today is as good as any other."

The cold, callous way he delivered those words only added to their impact. A thousand questions begged me to ask them but, in the end, there was only one that mattered.

"Why?" I swiped at the tears that insisted on spilling over my eyelids. I knew Corinne was enjoying this.

"Why?" Will repeated. "Difficult question to answer. I have always had questions about my life. You wouldn't understand, but being adopted and not knowing either biological parent you're bound to have questions. Then I came here and met Corinne. She understands. She has had the same questions. Now, finally, both of us are discovering the answers… Then there's…" He nodded in the direction of the library, but did he mean that?

Laurence interrupted before I could pursue it. "When were you thinking of telling me, Corinne? I thought we had something."

She blinked at him "Really? Oh well, never mind. You'll soon get over it. It was just a fling, Laurence. That's all. A harmless fling. Fun for a while but…I've found what I was looking for."

"What do you mean, Will?" I asked. "You said you were finding the answers. What answers?"

At that moment a vehicle pulled up outside. It must be after two o'clock. Mick would be here with Trevor, expecting to get on with their work. How could I act like nothing had happened? The doorbell rang. Clearly someone had to answer it but I couldn't get my feet to work. I felt numb.

Laurence launched into a full tirade of accusations. Any moment now and he would hit Will. Well, he could give him one from me too.

The bell rang again and the sound of it seemed to kick my unresponsive limbs into action. I left them to it and went to let Mick in. His face was white and his eyes wide. There was no sign of Trevor.

"What's wrong?" I asked, ushering him into the kitchen. The raised voices from the living room were reaching fever pitch but Mick appeared not to even hear them. I motioned him to sit at the kitchen table. His hands were shaking. I offered him coffee but he accepted a glass of water instead.

Finally, he spoke. "Trevor's missing, and his mother and me… We think something's happened to him."

I sat down adjacent to him. "When did you last see him?"

"It were yesterday. After we finished up here. I decided I'd use the opportunity to catch up with me accounts and Trevor…" His voice broke. "He said it were such a lovely day he wanted to go up on the moors. Have a walk in the sunshine. Maybe go over to the old abbey. He loved exploring up there. Found a curlew's nest there once. He used to go and watch the chicks having their first flying lessons." Mick took a sip of water. "I dropped him off a couple of hundred yards from the ruins and went on my way. He's a great walker is Trevor and it was broad daylight. Everyone knows him around here and anyone would have given him a lift back if they'd seen him on the road. And I told him to ring if he wanted picking up. That's when we both thought he had his phone with him. I didn't think anything of it for a couple of hours, but once it started to get dark, me and my wife started to get concerned. We phoned his mam and she said she hadn't heard from him and assumed he was with me so, while she was on the phone, my wife tried calling him. Not for the first time I might add. But this time, we could hear his phone ringing. He'd left it in his room. His mam hadn't heard it the previous times because she was downstairs. It just so happened she'd gone up to the bathroom when I called this time. I went straight back to the moor where I'd left him and started to search. By now we were losing the light. I hadn't a chance in hell of finding him if he was injured and unconscious so I drove to the pub. Five minutes after that around twenty of the locals were amassing up there with flashlights and sticks. He's classed as vulnerable so the police came out pretty much straightaway but we had to abandon the search then because it was too dark. They resumed this morning and…"

He broke down. I handed him kitchen roll to dry his tears and waited. The angry row seemed to have moved on from the living room but I hadn't the time or inclination to investigate. Mick needed to get this out and I needed to hear it.

After a few minutes, he dried his eyes. He began clutching and plucking at the piece of damp kitchen roll as he spoke. "They started again at first light and that's when they found… They found blood. Great splashes of it, over a patch of the old wall of the abbey. It looked like someone had attacked another person or animal but there was no one around. Then they found tire marks. Fresh ones. Now they think he may have been kidnapped and abducted."

"Oh my God, Mick." I put my arms around him and let him sob on my shoulder. Suddenly all my problems slipped into perspective. A faithless husband was nothing compared to the potential loss of this young lad.

When he had recovered himself a little, Mick spoke again. "I hope I didn't upset your husband when I phoned, but I had to know if Trevor had been here. He thought the world of you, Mrs. Clarke. He said you were the only one who would listen to him and believe what he said. He could talk to you because you both shared the…whatever it is in this place. He said there was something he wanted to tell you. Something he was going to tell you today. He said he couldn't before because he had only just worked it all out. I wish I'd listened to him. Got him to tell me what it was. But I just laughed it off as usual. Trevor and his funny little ways. Such an imagination." Back came the tears.

"You've no idea at all what he wanted to tell me?"

Mick shook his head. "He wouldn't tell me, would he? Nor his mam or any of his family. You're the only one he could talk to about this stuff. All he told me was it was about the house and he wanted to warn you. I told your husband that. He didn't seem too pleased. If only he'd felt he could tell us. Who's done this? What have they done with him? Where is he? I swear I'll listen in future. If they'd just bring him back."

I suddenly realized it had gone quiet out there. I listened. Nothing. "Just sit here and I'll be back shortly," I said. I dashed into the living room. Two of the occasional tables were upended and the rest of the furniture was in disarray. There was no one there. I left and made straight for the library. The first thing I saw was the old door pushed further aside, revealing the hole in the wall in its entirety.

I raced over, stood at the top of the steps and called. My voice echoed. I heard scuffles below.

"Will? Leah? Laurence? Are you down there?"

Flashes of light danced against the walls of the downstairs room. Footsteps. Two sets by the sound of it. Moving closer.

The beams from their combined flashlights blinded me. I stepped back and tripped, fell. I scrambled to get back on my feet but by now they were there. One on either side of me. Will and Corinne. They grabbed one arm each and dragged me up.

Will pressed his lips close to my ear. "No point in struggling now, Di. Come down with us."

"What's going on here? What are you doing?" I tried to scream but Corinne anticipated me and backhanded my mouth. The force of it jarred my brain. I tasted blood. Before I could try again, she had lowered her flashlight on the ground and anchored her hand firmly over my mouth. The woman was strong.

Together they dragged me down the steps and threw me on the cold, dank floor. My ankle struck the iron ring and I saw I wasn't alone. Corinne moved to the altar and began lighting candles. The room gradually became brighter. In a few seconds, I took in the scene. Laurence lay unconscious but unshackled close by me. On the other side of me, Leah's ankles were bound by the rusting restraints. Blood was dripping from her nose, which was bent at an odd angle. Her eyes were closed and I couldn't tell if she was breathing or not. Laurence faced away from me. His knuckles were skinned and his suit jacket torn. I couldn't see any other injuries but he didn't move.

"What are you doing, Will?" I asked. "I don't understand any of this."

The stranger I had given my heart to stared contemptuously down at me. "It's really very simple, Diana. Corinne and I were always meant to be together. I knew it from the moment I met her. I always knew I wasn't living the life mapped out for me and then one day, driving past this house it hit me. I reversed the car back up the road. The place drew me in. I walked all around it, drinking in its aura, seeing visions I had never imagined. And at the center of it, the man history records as Brother Alfred because they couldn't pronounce his real name. Afagddu ap Llewellyn. I didn't know the name then, or any details of what this place was, but it came into my head so when Corinne first mentioned it when we met that day in the estate agents, it was like a veil dropped and everything became clear. I realized where my destiny lay. Who I really am. Who *she* is."

A call sounded from above. Mick.

"Are you down there?"

"Call the police, Mick," I yelled before Corinne delivered another of her knockout punches.

Chapter Fifteen

The next thing I realized, I was coming to with a ferociously throbbing head and jaw. I raised my hand to my face and didn't like what I felt. No broken bones but there was already swelling. Goodness alone knew how long I'd been out. I tried to sit up. My head swam. Then I felt a movement next to me. Laurence.

"Thank God you're awake. I thought she'd done for you," he said. He touched my shoulder. "Do you think you can stand?"

I nodded but looked around me in the flickering candlelight before I attempted anything.

"They're not here, but they'll be back at any moment. I've been conscious since before they brought you down here. I knew I couldn't take them alone but together? It may be our only chance before they shut us in here, or worse."

"How could it be worse?"

He nodded over at the altar. "Look under there and you'll find out what happened to Trevor and, I'm afraid, his uncle joined him a few minutes ago."

"Mick? Oh no..."

"Shush. Don't make too much noise. I don't know where they are or if they can hear us. You told Mick to call the police. They couldn't risk that."

"We have to get out of here."

"I know. But we must be canny about it. We have to kill them, Diana. It's the only way."

The noise of footsteps above our heads. "Play dead," Laurence whispered. "We need some element of surprise."

I froze. Corinne's high heels clattered down the steps. She approached and I held my breath. From nearby, I heard a shuffling and then Will's voice. "Leah's dead."

"Are you sure?" Corinne could have been discussing the price of meat.

There was a pause. "Yep. No pulse. Pupils fixed and dilated as they say in all the best medical dramas."

Corinne giggled. "She would have been trouble. That's why I had to get her here. It's the only place I could be sure of finishing her off properly."

"There's always the abbey."

"No. It doesn't work anymore. I feel nothing there now. Nothing. When I was a child, yes, the atmosphere was full of Afagddu and Matilda's essence. I drew strength from it. Now it feels empty. Drained. All the power is concentrated right here. I think it happened when this place was reopened. It drew the spirit. Leah sensed it too."

"Interfering bitch. She was supposed to be a charlatan. Not the real fucking thing." I heard a thud. Will was no doubt kicking Leah's body.

"Leave her," Corinne said. "She's unimportant now. Come here."

More shuffling followed by the distinctive sound of kissing.

"Mm," Will said. "Where have you been all my life?"

"Waiting for you to realize who you really were."

"Imagine if I'd never found out."

"Oh you would. Afagddu has his ways, and so does Matilda. Just ask Lynn Schofield. Except you can't."

"She's the one who murdered her husband, baby and then killed herself."

"Not quite. When they were found, Peter, the husband, had a knife wound to the heart and Lynn lay in a pool of blood, the baby between her legs, still attached apparently. By some miracle it—he—was still alive. They concluded Lynn killed her husband with a kitchen knife and then slashed her own wrists, all while she was in labor or in the immediate aftermath of the birth. They hushed that bit up. About the baby. He was adopted but it was all kept quiet."

"When was this?"

"Twenty-eight years ago. I told you the place had been empty since then. I was born just down the road quite possibly at the very moment Matilda's spirit left Lynn's body in search of a new host. What better vessel than a newborn?"

"Afagddu had to wait a little longer," Will said. "Until the first time we discovered this room. What a day of revelation that was."

My heart was pounding. I wanted to leap up, kill them both. At that moment I didn't care that they were both possessed by evil entities that could do who knew what to me.

Will moved closer. I could sense him not six inches away from me. "We have unfinished business here." He poked my foot with his. So now I was merely a nuisance piece of garbage to be disposed of.

"We need to start the ceremony," Corinne said.

"Should we shackle them?" Will asked.

"They're both out cold. Besides, the only shackles that still work are secured to Leah's ankles and there's no time to start messing with those now. We need to sacrifice, and then be joined in the ceremony so that Afagddu and Matilda may live once more."

"And finally we get to consummate our union. It's been torture these past weeks, being so close to you and not able to do more than kiss you."

Corinne laughed. "Oh, you've done a little more than kissing, Will."

Will's laugh made me want to kill him. "And so have you. But finally we get to really make love. Right here. Naked. On *his* altar."

"After we take care of business. I'll move the candles onto the floor. Make room."

"I could take you right now."

"Oh no you don't. Come on, let's get her up on the altar, strip her naked—I'll leave that to you—and then summon our lord and master."

Strong arms grabbed me. I lashed out instinctively. Why didn't Laurence move? I struggled, screamed. Will slapped my face hard. It stopped me but only for a few seconds. Sufficient though for Corinne to slip something over my mouth to stifle my cries. It was old fabric and tasted foul. Bitter and sour and something I couldn't determine. Earth maybe. They threw me onto the altar.

"Hold her down," Will ordered as I kicked out, but Corinne wasn't letting me get away. The woman climbed onto the altar and sat astride me, ripping my shirt open. Between them, they stripped me naked in seconds, leaving me in agony from skin burns and abrasions where they had hit me, ripped my underclothes off and now forced my legs open.

In flashes, I saw the girl I had witnessed in my spirit state that night. In one moment, I was seeing her as an observer, in the next I *was* her, looking out at my violators. Sometimes they were Will and Corinne. At others, the bearded monk with the hideous grin that must be Afagddu, and a nun whose face I had never seen before but who gazed at my nakedness with a mixture of lust and contempt.

Then the chanting began. Two voices, rising in pitch and volume. More joined them. Corinne flipped me over and bound my wrists and ankles, ignoring my struggles to kick free. Then, in the flickering candlelight I caught a glimpse of a long, wicked-looking blade. The voices were at fever pitch now. My visions of the girl and me raveled and unraveled, wove, unwove, merged and then, out of the corner of my eye, I saw the beast Leah had known was there. It stayed on the very periphery of my vision and I knew that *there* was its natural home. Lurking, almost out of sight. Somehow I knew that in its current state it could do relatively little harm, but released to fill my field of vision, its power would reach its zenith. And that would be the end of me.

"It's almost time," Corinne cried. "He's here."

Smoke, fire, the sickening smell of sulfur. I closed my eyes and prayed for a swift, merciful end.

But it didn't come.

I braced myself. Tried to pray.

Another voice—deep and resonant—swelled and smothered the hysterical chanting. Screams. I had never heard Will scream before, but I heard it now. The vicious grip on my body vanished. Warm hands touched my ankles. The new voice provided its own chant in Latin. I lay still, sensing that the owner of *this* voice, *these* hands, had come to save me.

One slice of a sharp blade and the ropes that bound my feet were released. Another and my hands were free.

Still the man's chanting continued, only now, his was the lone voice. I turned over and stared straight into Laurence's eyes. His face was splattered with blood. And, as he moved, he dragged his right leg. More blood saturated the fabric of his torn trousers on that leg right down to his ankle.

On the floor, the bodies of Will and Corinne lay sprawled, their throats sliced cleanly. Next to them, a dagger, the blade I had seen minutes earlier.

"They got careless," he said, a smile lighting up his bloodied face for a moment. "They assumed I was either dead or well out of it. Big mistake. While they were preoccupied with getting you under control, I was able to grab their blade and fortunately all those fencing lessons at that fancy school my parents spent so much money on paid off for once. Now, come on, we haven't any time to waste. We've got to get as far away from here as possible before anyone comes looking for these people. The police are already searching for Trevor. It's only a matter of time before they get here and then they'll find a whole lot of other folk they didn't even know were gone."

"But surely we can explain—"

He silenced me with a finger over my mouth. "Don't even go there, Diana. Assuming they believe our story—even if we leave out all reference to the supernatural—there's the small matter of the spirits of Afagddu and Matilda. Now I don't know how long it takes a spirit to depart the body but it's not going to be long. Then they will be searching for new hosts. Hopefully they can't travel too far. They seem to have kept it local up to now. We have to move and I think… it's probably best if you put some clothes on and probably a face mask would be good—or a snood if you have one. Your face is…" He frowned.

"You can wear something of Will's. I'm sorry but it's the best I can do."

"Okay, but come on, we have to hurry. No time to pack a suitcase. Wash quickly. No long showers, just enough to get the worst off. I'll do the same. We don't want to attract attention to ourselves by looking like Freddy Krueger."

I found I could walk better than Laurence and it was clear I would be doing the driving too. His right leg was only superficially wounded—most of the blood had emanated from Corinne and Will—but he had twisted his ankle on the fall down the steps when Corinne and Will pushed him.

We were out of the house in under ten minutes; on the way out I had grabbed the jacket Will had discarded. His wallet was tucked into an inside pocket.

Laurence's car was a 4x4, similar to ours, for which I was thankful. At least we shouldn't get stuck in any potholes and would be able to get up some speed.

"Where are we going?" I asked as I headed us out towards Leeds.

"Get onto the A1(M). We're headed for the far north of Scotland. It's easier to get lost up there. New identities. We can plan a new life. This car doesn't have GPS and without phones we won't be easy to track."

"What about CCTV…your registration plates?"

"Don't worry. Drive carefully. Stop when I tell you because I'll need to make a quick phone call and I know where there's a public call box."

We drove mostly in silence until Laurence told me to pull over. The call box was in a quiet country lane on the edge of a sleepy village. Laurence reached into the glove compartment and removed a small bag of coins. "Back in a sec," he said and scrambled, painfully out of the car.

He was back in a few minutes. "Drive back to the main road and carry on north. We're meeting up with a friend of mine. He owns a garage and owes me a favor or two. I put him onto a sweet opportunity a couple of years ago and his small one-man business has grown a little since then." Judging by his laugh I gathered a little meant a whole lot. I didn't ask. As we went on, I realized how little I knew about the man to whom I was entrusting my life. But hadn't he come through for me? Without him I would be lying dead in that revolting room.

I told myself that more than once on our mostly silent journey. The next stop was close to a service station but just far enough away to be hidden by trees and off the road. Once again, he told me to wait in the car but, by now, a call of nature sent me dashing behind a convenient oak tree while the two men busied themselves with changing the number plates. By the time I returned, the friend was busy burying the old ones some distance off.

"No one will be finding those in a hurry," Laurence said. "Come on, let's go."

He whistled and waved at his friend who paused in his digging and waved back. Once again we set off, rejoined the main road and sped off up to Scotland.

Not far from Inverness, I glanced at the petrol gauge. "We need to fill up."

"We'll pull in at the next service station. You're going to have to do it though."

"Great, but what do I pay with? I forgot to bring any money or cards with me."

"You couldn't have used cards if you had. Too traceable. I, on the other hand…" He fiddled in the pocket of Will's jacket and withdrew his wallet. "We have precisely…" he counted. "Two hundred and eighty-five pounds here. Plus change. Did he usually carry so much cash around with him?"

"It depended. He was a bit old school. Preferred to pay cash, even these days."

"Well God bless the old school," Laurence said and I actually laughed. It was then I realized that my love for Will had evaporated or maybe it was simply numbed by what he had done and how he had intended to kill me. Now when I thought of him, I only felt anger and resentment. Maybe that was wrong of me. Before that house, he had been a different person. He hadn't asked to be possessed by evil, but I couldn't forgive him. Not yet. Maybe one day. They say time heals all, don't they?

It was pitch dark by the time we reached Scotland's north-easternmost county of Caithness. It seemed barren, empty, devoid of life. We traveled miles with hardly a sign of human habitation although I ventured to suggest it might be different in daylight.

"Only a little," Laurence said. "Then you can really see how isolated this place is. It's perfect for us of course. A chance to rest, heal and recover until we're ready to decide where we go next."

"We won't be going far on two hundred quid," I said.

"Don't worry. We won't have to get by on that."

"How? Or perhaps I shouldn't ask."

"Wise move," Laurence said. He touched my hand on the steering wheel. "It's okay. Nothing for you to worry about. I'll come clean with you. I've done some…shall we say…questionable stuff in the past. A bit of trading that wasn't entirely kosher. I have a few offshore bank accounts. Enough to provide a comfortable cushion until we're well established under our new identities in some friendly South American country. I also know a few people and I have a few more favors to call in. One of them lives about twenty miles from where we are now. He'll put us up for a couple of weeks, get us kitted out with new passports and so forth for which I will repay him handsomely and then off we go. Nice chap, you'll like him. He's an artist. Paints gorgeous watercolors."

Laurence was right. I did like Josh. His house was down a dirt track, nothing from the outside but inside it was a modern interior designer's dream with its chrome, glass and minimalist décor. His own paintings adorned the walls. Swirls of black, gray and white, suggestive of the gigantic storms that must frequently batter this countryside. I asked no questions. Whatever dodgy dealings Laurence was, or had been, involved in were nothing to do with me and, I reasoned, the less I knew about them, the better. All that mattered was that, for now at least, I was safe.

When the time came to leave, I was sad to go. The bleak awesomeness of Caithness had worked its way into my psyche. I suggested we stay but Laurence said it wasn't wise. We needed to put an ocean between us and not only the police but whatever remained of

Afagddu and Matilda. I often thought of the bodies we had left behind. They would have been found within a very short time and we would be on a "Persons of Interest" list at the very least. Oh, who was I kidding? We would be their "most wanted" in relation to the murders. I often wondered what would have happened if we had stayed. Too late now of course. Josh didn't have a television or internet. He lived his life off grid and seemed far more content as a result of it. Maybe that was a lesson for the future. I have certainly found, as time has passed, I have missed contact with the outside world and especially the often toxic online variety, less and less.

The inevitable day has dawned. Our last in the UK. We have passports, an array of tickets for various modes of transport, US dollars, clothes, credit cards with our new identities, and neither one of us looks anything like we did when we arrived—or even before we were beaten up. It's amazing what a radical change of hair color and style can achieve, and Laurence's beard suits him. We have grown closer over the nearly six weeks we have spent in Josh's house. I can now say that I think we may be a couple. That's not very definite, is it? Some days I absolutely believe we are who it says on our passports—Phil Ramsey and Tina Ramsey—a married couple five years older than our actual ages. Then there are other days when I'm not so sure. There's a look in Laurence's eyes sometimes... But then he smiles and we laugh and pour some more wine.

We say our tearful (in my case) goodbyes to Josh and set off in his car which we'll leave at his friend's private airstrip. From there, the same friend will fly us to somewhere in Ireland where our adventure truly begins. I don't know exactly where we will end up. Laurence—I mean, Phil, because I must get used to calling him that from now on—said it's best I only know one leg of the journey at a time. If we should get caught, the less I know the better. I can then claim he kidnapped me. Not that I would. But that's the way he wants it. I could sneak a peek at the tickets but to be honest, I don't really care where we go. As long as Matilda and Afagddu can't find us, and the way they will do that is by getting into our heads. So, he's right. The less I know, the better. As for the police? They don't frighten me. They're human. Humans I can deal with. The supernatural? Now that's something else entirely.

I can see the small white 'plane, sitting, waiting for us. Phil drives up to it. We get out. His limp is a thing of the past these days and, as I watch him retrieve our suitcases out of the back of the car, I feel a rush of warmth. He really is a good-looking man. And when he smiles, I melt.

If only that smile made it all the way up to his eyes.

If only there wasn't that niggling voice inside me:

Don't trust him.

Epilog

Matilda's Retreat—Two years later

The woman stares at the house, her feet firmly planted against the buffeting moorland wind that howls its loneliness all around her.

Her gaze travels up to the windows—dark, like closed eyes, shuttered against the world. A few yards away, a solitary sheep rears up, and backs away as if it has strayed too close to the solid walls. It bleats its rage, catches the woman's eye and stares at her, just for a moment. Then it's off at a gallop, as if fearful it can't get away far or fast enough.

A trace of a smile crosses the woman's face as she makes her halting way up to the door and turns the handle. It should be locked but it gives at her touch and she enters.

Inside, all is still, bar the creak of old timbers. The smell is of age, dust and emptiness.

The woman gazes all around her, drinking in the atmosphere she has missed for so long. She feels the familiar ethereal embrace and knows she is welcome.

"I have come back, my lord," she says, "after all these years. You called me and I obeyed."

A whispered sigh courses along the deserted hallways, through the empty rooms until it finds her, caresses her and enfolds her in a lover's embrace. Then, it moves on, into the library.

Silently, Jacqueline Le Pellier follows.

Acknowledgments

As always, my heartfelt thanks go to Julia Kavan, my friend and fellow writer, who first read *Matilda's Retreat* when it was a rather long short story called, simply, *The House on the Moor*. In that incarnation, it was always too lengthy for magazine editors to consider and, in any case, there was clearly more of its story to tell. Once it had grown to its current length, off it went back to her and, again, she shared her valuable insights and incredible talent for homing in on the inconsistencies and flaws like a heatseeking missile. Any lingering nonsense is entirely of my own making.

Massive thanks to David Wilson and David Dodd. I am indebted to them for breathing new life into my back catalog and for launching my originals—like *Matilda's Retreat*—on an unsuspecting public. Crossroad Press is a fabulous publisher to work with and it is always a pleasure.

Thanks and a special mention go to my partners in crime—the group we call The Shippy Writers, for reasons embedded in the annals of our history. We meet once per month and sometimes we even get around to discussing writerly pursuits. We even managed to produce our first anthology. *Chimera: An Anthology* is out now and profits go to Rescue Me—a small animal charity based on Merseyside which first introduced Colin and me to a certain black cat, Serafina. You can find the fruit of our labors on Amazon in eBook and in print.

My husband, Colin, deserves a medal for all he puts up with—lugging shedloads of books to festivals and horror markets is only part of it. He's the unsung hero of so much of my life and also the only one prepared to get up at some ungodly hour to cater to the whims of our aforementioned feline autocrat.

And thank you to *you*. You've made it to the end of my latest novella unscathed (I hope). Your tenacity is much appreciated. I hope you enjoyed the experience and will join me for many more forays into houses we really shouldn't enter and down staircases from which we may never emerge.

Catherine Cavendish,
Southport, U.K.

About the Author

Following a varied career in sales, advertising and career guidance, Catherine Cavendish is now the full-time author of a number of paranormal, ghostly and Gothic horror novels and novellas.

Her novels include: *The Stones of Landane, Those Who Dwell in Mordenhyrst Hall, The After-Death of Caroline Rand, Nemesis of the Gods trilogy: Wrath of the Ancients, Waking the Ancients,* and *Damned by the Ancients, Dark Observation, In Darkness, Shadows Breathe, The Garden of Bewitchment. The Haunting of Henderson Close, The Devil's Serenade, The Pendle Curse* and *Saving Grace Devine.*

The Crow Witch and Other Conjurings is a collection of her previously published and brand new short stories.

Her novellas include: *The Darkest Veil, Linden Manor, Cold Revenge, Miss Abigail's Room, The Demons of Cambian Street, Dark Avenging Angel, The Devil Inside Her,* and *The Second Wife.*

She lives by the sea in Southport, England with her long-suffering husband, and a black cat called Serafina who has never forgotten that her species used to be worshipped in ancient Egypt. She sees no reason why that practice should not continue.

You can connect with Cat here:

Website: catherinecavendish.com/
Facebook: facebook.com/CatherineCavendishWriter
X (formerly Twitter): twitter.com/Cat_Cavendish
Instagram: instagram.com/catcavendish/
Tik Tok: catcavendish
Bluesky @catcavendish.bsky.social

CROSSROAD
PRESS

www.ingramcontent.com/pod-product-compliance
Lightning Source LLC
LaVergne TN
LVHW091001080826
845145LV00003B/1086
* 9 7 8 1 6 3 7 8 9 3 4 9 4 *